FLYING IN
PLACE

◇
◆
◇

Susan Palwick

FLYING IN PLACE

SUSAN PALWICK

A TOM DOHERTY ASSOCIATES BOOK
NEW YORK

This is a work of fiction. All the characters and events portrayed in this book are fictitious, and any resemblance to real people or events is purely coincidental.

FLYING IN PLACE

A Tor Book
Published by Tom Doherty Associates, Inc.
175 Fifth Avenue
New York, N.Y. 10010

Library of Congress Cataloging-in-Publication Data

Palwick, Susan.
Flying in Place / by Susan Palwick.—1st ed.
p. cm.
"TOR book"—T.p. verso.
ISBN 0-312-85183-9
I. Title.
PS3566.A554C47 1992
813'.54—dc20 90-27351
CIP

Printed in the United States of America

First edition: May 1992

0 9 8 7 6 5 4 3 2 1

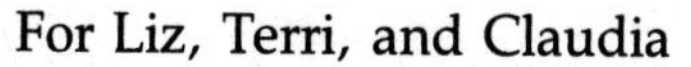

For Liz, Terri, and Claudia

AUTHOR'S NOTE

For their support, suggestions, and technical assistance, I'd like to thank Ellen Kushner, Gary Meyer, Gail Meyers, Patrick Nielsen Hayden, Teresa Nielsen Hayden, Helen Palwick, Liz and Lloyd Palwick-Goebel, Sylvia Rosenfeld, Barbara Rozen, Alex Silverman, Valerie Smith, and Terri Windling.

Although Pamela quotes briefly from Christina Rossetti's "Goblin Market," *Hamlet*, T. S. Eliot's "Journey of the Magi" and Auden's "In Memory of W. B. Yeats," most of her poetic rhetoric is paraphrased from Tennyson's "In Memoriam A.H.H."

FLYING IN PLACE

◆ ◇ ◆

BRET FOUND the letters today. I'd forgotten to lock the door to my study, and Nancy got in. I hadn't locked the desk because I'm usually so careful about locking the door, so Nancy—large for her age, and with the determined energy of all toddlers—scaled my writing chair and dug a group of letters out of one of the cubbyholes. She was eating pieces of correspondence by the time Bret found her. "Thank God you use blue felt-tip and not red," he told me later, "or I'd have thought she was dying."

I'd gotten home to find a freshly scrubbed Nancy nursing a bottle of apple juice, and Bret on the floor of the study, gingerly sorting pieces of blue-smeared paper. "Hi," he said when he saw me. "She was eating these. I haven't been reading them, really I haven't, I'm just trying to put them back together—"

"It's okay," I said. My drive home through autumn foliage had soothed me, and thirty feet from my study window shone the Delaware River, bright waterfalls chattering on rocks. We're too high here for the river to be tranquil, but it's usually merry. It reminds me of Nancy. "I trust you."

Bret scratched his nose, getting ink on it, and said, "I know you don't want anybody in here."

"It's okay," I said. "I forgot to lock the door." I'd

remembered that I'd forgotten to lock the door as soon as I was irrevocably ensconced in the supermarket checkout line, and all the way home, as the car swept aside falling leaves, I'd been wondering what would happen. I'd never forgotten to lock the door before. "It's probably because I trust you."

Bret looked at the pieces of paper surrounding him. Nancy actually hadn't eaten much, maybe a year's worth out of fifteen. I picked up one of the torn sheets, which recorded a fragment of my first vacation with Bret. A good year: the kid couldn't be faulted for her taste. "Do you trust me enough to tell me what they are?" Bret asked.

"Letters," I said, and looked away from him, out at the river. Water has always calmed me.

"Unmailed?"

"They're to my sister."

"Really," Bret said, not happily. In my peripheral vision, I saw him scratch his nose again. "What about?"

"Myself. You, Nancy. Like a journal, really."

"Oh," he said. "You write her letters even though you never knew her? Or because you never knew her? Emma?"

You didn't lock the door, I told myself firmly, finally failing to be comforted by the river, and said, "I knew her. I did."

"How? When?"

"She visited me," I said carefully, looking back at Bret, "when I was twelve. When we were both twelve."

Bret shook his head and said just as carefully, "How'd she get there? I mean, she couldn't exactly have walked. Could she?"

If you told Myrna you can tell Bret, I told myself. He's your husband. He knows you're not crazy. You love him. You didn't lock the door. "Actually," I said, "the first time I saw her she was doing cartwheels."

Bret started to smile, and evidently thought better of it. Nancy, finished with her juice, discarded the bottle and let out a joyous shriek; Bret reached out and retrieved the bottle, beating it against his thigh in a tattoo that told me how tense he was, despite his seeming calm. "Cartwheels. Okay. Where?"

I closed my eyes, remembering the pre-dawn grayness of that April Wisconsin morning, the ranks of shadows cast on the walls by the venetian blinds, row upon row of thin horizontal bars, and how I'd risen out of my body to try to get away from them, away from the bars and the grayness and the noise. My mother said that dawn was the noisiest time of day because of the birds, but birdsong wasn't the sound I dreaded. Breathing was.

"Emma?" Bret asked gently. "Where was she doing cartwheels?"

I swallowed. Talking hadn't been this difficult for years. "On my bedroom ceiling."

◆ ◇ ◆

I RECOGNIZED HER right away. I probably would have recognized her even if her picture hadn't been hanging all over the house, because she'd inherited our parents' best features, the ones I'd always wanted: Mom's blue eyes and flowing auburn hair, my father's roman nose and firm chin. I'd gotten the leftovers: Mom's gap teeth and propensity to freckle at the slightest hint of sunlight, my father's frizzy brown curls and big ears. My tendency to fat must have been a recessive trait from several generations back, because neither of my parents was about to claim it.

"Ginny was light as a bird," my mother often said with a sigh. She kept Ginny's favorite nightgown—a frilly affair with lots of lace and ribbons—carefully preserved in a cedar chest, and often told me that Ginny was prettier in that nightgown than most little girls were in party dresses. I always wore pajamas. My mother hated pajamas.

To my surprise, Ginny was wearing a pair of yellow cotton pajamas with Snoopy on them, which must have made doing cartwheels a lot easier. I'd been hovering next to the ceiling, counting the lilac blossoms on the tree outside my window, when she came tumbling through the wall my bedroom shared with hers. Her red-gold curls were mussed from her calisthenics, but the cartwheels were perfect. She didn't seem to know I was there, but she looked solid enough; to my satisfaction, she didn't even have a halo.

I'd only learned how to leave my body a few weeks before, after years of feigned sleep, and I was still surprised at how easy it was: one of those skills that seems impossible at first but quickly becomes second nature, like tying your shoes. Because I wasn't in my body, I could define directions any way I wanted to. I rotated so that my feet were on the ceiling and the breathing was coming from over my head. As always, I tried not to pay attention to it, but today it was louder than usual and counting flowers hadn't been helping, so Ginny was a welcome distraction. She reached the opposite wall and I wondered if she'd go through it, into my parents' room—Mom would really love that—but instead she turned and started doing cartwheels in the other direction, coming back towards me.

"Hi," I said. "What are you doing here?"

She stopped and stood up—which meant that her feet were planted on the ceiling like mine—and squinted at me, frowning, her head cocked to one side. "Cartwheels," she said. The breathing sounded like a hurricane now, but if Ginny heard it she didn't let on. Mom never heard anything either; that must have been another congenital tendency. I may have been fat, but at least I wasn't deaf.

"You can't do cartwheels," I told her. I'd never been able to do cartwheels, no matter what I was wearing. "You aren't even supposed to be here. You're dead. Go back to your own room, where you belong."

"But I am supposed to be here," she said. "I wouldn't be here if I weren't supposed to be here."

"That's called circular logic," I told her, "but I grade easier than Mom does so I'll let you pass this time, if you tell me why you're here."

She was there to distract me from the breathing; it was easy enough to figure that out. Maybe she'd be able to teach me how to go through walls too, and then I'd finally be able to get into her room. The door had been locked for as long as I could remember. Mom didn't want anybody in there and my father acted like the room didn't exist at all, and if the key was still around somewhere I sure hadn't been able to find it. I'd have bet all my Nancy Drew books that Ginny's room was nicer than mine.

"I don't know why I'm here," Ginny said. She took a piece of her hair and put it in her mouth, biting at the ends the way Mom always told me not to do. Her hands were even smaller than I'd expected, the fingers like little sticks with knobs on them, something out of Hansel and Gretel. You could break those fingers without even trying. "I can't remember. I can't even remember who I am."

"You're nobody," I said, disgusted. She wasn't distracting me very well; I could still hear the breathing, heavy as waves crashing on a beach. What good was being out of my body, if I couldn't get away from the breathing? "You're a ghost."

"I am? But ghosts used to be people. Didn't I used to be somebody? I can't—"

"Remember," I said. "For somebody who made high honor roll every marking period of her life your brain's really gone soft, you know that? Does being dead do that to everybody?"

Her face brightened. "Ha! See? You *do* know who I was!"

"Are you kidding? How could I not know who you are? It's not like Mom would ever let me forget it! Most kids get Seuss stories at bedtime: I've gotten Ginny stories, as long as I can remember—"

"Ginny," she said, and hugged herself. "That's right! I remember! I had one of those bracelets with the little beads that said Ginny. And birthday cakes that said Ginny. And books—a lot of books with brown paper covers, and I wrote Ginny on them. Thank you!"

She unclasped herself and took a few dancing steps towards me like she was going to hug me, but I backed off and she stopped short, frowning. I hoped she was hurt. I wanted her to be hurt.

"That's right: Ginny, my perfect sister, the one who was skinnier than I am and smarter than I am and had better manners than I do. The one who had pretty thick curls instead of mouse-brown frizz. The one nobody ever laughed at in gym, because on top of getting straight A plusses she was a champion gymnast. So why did you come back, anyway? Heaven wasn't good enough for you? Didn't they worship you up there the way Mom does?"

"I already told you, I don't know!" There was the edge of a whine in her voice. Good. I was getting to her, then. She scowled at me and said, "Are you dead, too? Why are you here, if you aren't dead?"

"Stupid ghost! You can't even hear it, can you?" I waved a hand over my head, in the direction of the floor, and Ginny looked where I was pointing and then back at me, so quickly I wasn't even sure she'd seen it. "It's your fault," I told her. "Because you went and died, and parts of Mom died when you did. Isn't that nice? Doesn't that make you feel good?"

She didn't say anything; just stared at me, both hands over her mouth. "Maybe that's why you had to come back," I said. "So you'd have to look at it. Maybe they think they made a mistake, letting you into heaven. Maybe they think you've got it too easy, sitting up there singing hymns all day."

She took her hands away from her mouth. "You're mean," she said, her voice breaking. She was crying, shining droplets rolling down her Ivory-Snow cheeks.

"That's right. I've got to be mean to somebody, and it might as well be you. You aren't even real."

Ginny put her arms around herself and hugged, rocking. "I am so! I'm as real as you are! I am, even if I can't remember anything!"

"No, you aren't, because you're dead. Anyway, I like being mean. I'm going to be mean some more, because I'm still alive and you aren't. Did you know that Mom wouldn't hold me for two weeks after I was born, because I wasn't you? She told me that once. It's not like I would have remembered it or anything, but she had to let me know. She puts flowers on your grave every month, every fourth Saturday no matter what the weather's like, even if it's twenty below zero—especially then, since you died in January. She won't go into your room, but she goes to the cemetery every month. Figure that one out. And she drags me with her so she can tell me more stories about you, so I'll be more like you—"

"But if you were like me you'd be dead," said Ginny, wiping her face with the back of one hand. Her tiny fingers were shaking like twigs in a winter wind. "She doesn't want that. I know she doesn't want that."

"I don't. If I died she could pretend I was beautiful. You're not as beautiful as she thinks you are, you know. You're too skinny."

"I know," she said simply, and even though I hated her I was ashamed. She really was as pretty as her picture;

she was so thin only because she'd been so sick before she died, battling pneumonia for weeks while Mom wept by her hospital bedside and my father, the omnipotent physician, railed at his inability to save her. I knew that story by heart. Once, before it had become so many words, it had even made me sad.

But it didn't matter what I told this apparition, because she wasn't real. I'd thought her up to distract me from the breathing, and if she made me feel bad I could send her away again. "Go away," I said. "Go back to wherever you came from. You're just a ghost. You're a ghost with no memory, and that's worse than nothing. What good are you, if you can't tell me anything I don't know?"

She shivered all over now. "I know lots you don't know."

I know something you don't know. Perfect Ginny, reduced to that game. "Prove it," I told her. "Tell me something important, something I couldn't know any other way. Tell me how to get into your room."

She put a lock of hair in her mouth, chewed on it thoughtfully, blinked, and shivered again. "Aunt Donna and I have the same pajamas."

"Huh? That's not what I asked you! Anyway, you can't even remember names, stupid. You mean Aunt Diane, Dad's sister in Ohio—"

"Aunt Donna," she repeated.

"I don't *have* an Aunt Donna!"

"We bought them at Macy's," she said, wiping her eyes with the back of her hand again. She looked relieved. "So I'd have something from the store even though I couldn't go to the parade. I think that's why I'm here. To tell you that." And then she turned and walked through the wall again, back into the place I'd never been allowed to go, and I was alone with the lilacs and the venetian blinds. The breathing had stopped, finally. When I craned my head up at the bed I could see my ugly fat body lying there like a rag doll someone had tossed aside. It was time for me to go back, so I could get up and eat breakfast and go to school.

◆ ◇ ◆

GETTING BACK in was harder than it had been the other times, as if my body were a piece of clothing that had shrunk in the wash. When I finally made it I felt a searing pain between my legs and the warm stickiness of blood, and I knew why the breathing had been so loud.

He'd never done that before. He'd done plenty of other things, but never anything that would leave any kind of mark, and I'd never thought he'd treat me more carelessly than he'd treat one of his patients.

He was a meticulous surgeon. Everyone he worked with said so, and the most important people in town looked up to him. The local judge always sent us a crate of oranges for New Year's, because my father had done his prostate surgery. The mayor had invited us over for dinner after my father removed his five-year-old grandson's appendix.

Even people who disliked him respected him. My father loved to tell the story of how the chief pathologist at the hospital had postponed his gall bladder operation until my father could do it, although they'd hated each other for years. "You've earned your arrogance, Stewart. At least I won't be conscious to listen to you bragging about how elegantly you're cutting me open."

My father had answered, "No, but when you come to you'll have to listen to me bragging about how elegantly I sewed you back up."

By now, the anecdote was a family joke. Whenever he sliced a ham or turkey, my mother said, "At least it isn't conscious to listen to you bragging about how beautifully you're carving it." But here I was, bleeding. He never would have left a patient bleeding in bed.

"You mustn't ever tell anyone," he'd said the first few times he came into my bedroom at dawn, back when I was a very little girl, "because it would kill your mother if she found out that you do more for me than she does." He'd said it in that sincere, kind voice of his, and then he'd reached under my pajamas and pinched my nipples, hard, one after another.

But even at their hardest, the pinches only hurt for a moment, and doctors always did that, didn't they? The careful, compassionate hands saying, "This won't hurt a bit," and then the sudden pain of the shot, until finally you learn that "This won't hurt a bit" really means, "This will only hurt a little bit, for a moment, so that you won't hurt more later on."

I'd always thought of those pinches as inoculations, guarding against worse pain; and whatever pain he caused me, I certainly didn't want to find out what would happen if I told Mom or anyone else, any more than I wanted to find out what it felt like to have measles or polio or the pneumonia that had killed Ginny. If my mother knew, it would kill her; he'd said so clearly enough. Ginny's death had already killed the parts of Mom that would have kept him out of my room at dawn. If she found out and died completely—

No, I wasn't going to think about that. I had to think about good things instead, so I wouldn't get scared. I thought about all the people he'd saved, how he'd taught me to swim, how he always managed to carve out the faces I drew on Halloween pumpkins, no matter how complicated I made them.

It had become a ritual; each October 30 I drew the fanciest face I could, and each October 31 my father came home from the hospital wearing scrubs, gloves, and mask, and carrying a case of scalpels. For an hour or so, the kitchen would become an operating room. He wouldn't let me handle the scalpels because they were too sharp, but I helped him with everything else. "Light!" he'd tell me, and I'd shine the flashlight where he wanted it; "Swab!" and I'd wipe his forehead. The final two commands were always "Candle!" and "Matches!" and the operations were always successful. We won the town Jack O'Lantern contest every year.

Thinking about the pumpkins usually cheered me up, but today the scalpels only reminded me of the blood, so I thought about the balloons instead. When I was seven I'd been stuck in bed with the mumps, and my father had blown up rubber gloves and drawn faces on them with magic marker, so that they looked like grinning animals with stubby legs and tails. One of them broke when I touched it, and I started crying, but my father laughed and said, "Don't be upset, Emma. I can make another one, see?"

And he did. Because I'd been so little and sick,

watching a rubber glove become a happy animal had seemed magical. But today, thinking about my father blowing up balloons only reminded me of the breathing.

Eyes closed, I drank in lilac blossom and clutched handfuls of the pink and yellow woolen afghan Mom had started crocheting when she first found out she was pregnant with me. She'd stopped work on it three months later, when Ginny died, and hadn't finished it until the brutally cold winter when I was nine. I was careful only to touch the top third of it, which was softer and neater than the rest.

When I opened my eyes the clock said 6:02, almost time for breakfast; but when I sat up the pain nearly made me whimper, despite all the practice I'd had at silence. It was hard to walk without wincing, and the soft cotton of my bathrobe hurt my skin. I limped across the hall to the bathroom and ran a good hot shower. The pain would fade and the blood would wash off, but I was terrified that I might be going crazy. Only crazy people or people in books saw ghosts, and if I'd just dreamed up Ginny to keep me company, why had she said all those things that didn't make any sense?

I didn't have an Aunt Donna, and the Macy's parade was in New York and Mom wasn't about to let any child of hers set foot in that cesspool. The only time I'd ever been out of Wisconsin was at Christmas, when we always went to Ohio to see Aunt Diane, who owned a bunch of horses. I liked the horses a lot better than I liked Diane, who looked like a horse and seemed to believe that this put her on a par with British royalty. I had no idea what Diane wore in bed, but I was certain it wasn't Snoopy pajamas.

Thinking about all this in the shower reassured me, because it meant that maybe I wasn't crazy, even if I'd started seeing ghosts who said crazy things. By the time I got out of the shower I was ready to pretend that everything was fine. I'd just go to school, the way I always did.

But when I went back into my room the bloodstained sheets were in a heap on the floor, and my mother was putting clean ones on the bed. My father kept telling her she should hire a cleaning lady so she wouldn't have so much to do, but she said housework relaxed her. My private suspicion was that no one else's cleaning efforts could have met her standards. Certainly mine didn't.

I stood and watched her, admiring her grace and efficiency, wishing I could run out of the house before she turned around and saw me. What was I going to say when she asked me where the blood had come from? I'd taken his medicine like a good girl, and I'd never told anyone. I hadn't told even now, had I? He'd told. The blood he'd left had told; but I was frightened anyway.

If I could think of a way to make it sound poetic, maybe it wouldn't kill her. She'd told me that poetry had kept her alive after Ginny died, and at school she was infamous for alternating her grammar drills and vocabulary quizzes with lessons about Shakespeare and Tennyson. But she'd never yet given me an A in one of the poetry units. I was too good at grammar and vocabulary, and if I got anything higher than a B in English people would think she was playing favorites. She wouldn't let me switch teachers because she didn't think any of the others knew as much as she did, so she just marked me down as far as she could on anything that was open to interpretation.

No, poetry wouldn't have worked even if I'd had the time to come up with something clever. Maybe I could pretend I'd cut myself. I'd sneak back into the bathroom, where there were razors—

But I didn't have time for that either, because Mom finished folding the clean sheet over the blanket and tucked both of them under the mattress, and then she turned and saw me standing there. To my bewilderment, she smiled: one of those shy smiles people in movies give their first true love. She was really looking at me, for once, and she didn't even look disgusted.

"Well," she said, and took a step towards me, beaming. "Well, you've gotten your period. Congratulations."

I opened my mouth and closed it. "It's wonderful," she said, and she looked genuinely happy, and it made her as beautiful as any of the pictures I'd seen of Ginny. "It's a good thing, Emma, really it is. It means you're a woman, that you can have children when you want to and add to the sum of the world, your life bound up in tender lives; it means your body is strong and healthy and doing what it was designed to do. Don't ever be ashamed of that."

I swallowed. I didn't have to invent a poetic lie. She'd done it for me. What had I expected from someone who couldn't even hear the breathing? No wonder I'd started seeing ghosts, in a house where nothing was real anyway. "Oh," I said. "Well, I'm sorry about the sheets."

She shook her head. "Don t be. It's even a fitting season for it. All the secrets of the spring moved in the chambers of the blood. . . ." She laughed and said, "I guess it's too early in the morning to be quoting old Alfred, but don't worry about the sheets. It's happened to all of us."

I shuddered. Most of the time she yelled if I got butter on the tablecloth. "Yeah, I guess."

Normally she would have corrected me: "*Yes,* Emma, I *suppose* so." But this time she went on as if I hadn't said anything sloppy at all. "And you're younger than I was. I was thirteen when I got mine. You're only twelve. I've heard that girls—women—" she laughed again "—are getting it earlier now, because they're healthier. It's because of better nutrition."

Mom had always prided herself on feeding me well, even though it meant I was fatter than my blessèd sister. "Ginny was such a picky eater," Mom would say with a sigh as I polished off a heaping plate. "Light as a bird." It was some kind of test, as if even though she gave me gobs of food I was supposed to prove my purity and innocence by not eating it all. But I always did, like greedy Laura devouring the faerie fruit in "Goblin Market," that charming tale Mom had read me at bedtime when I was a little girl and demanded story books instead of anecdotes about Ginny. "Goblin Market" and *Peter Pan,* forbidden fruit and forbidden flight, evil little men and crocodiles lurking to claim the unwary—delightful stuff to dream of until dawn, when the breathing started.

"My mother didn't get it until she was fifteen," Mom said, still with that bashful smile, "so there must be something to the nutrition theory. Do you have cramps? How do you feel?"

"I feel fine," I said. My hands were shaking now, despite my efforts to control them. "How old was Ginny when she got her period, Mom?"

The smile disappeared in an instant, replaced by the familiar look of anguish and hatred. Ginny had died before she'd gotten her period, and I knew it, and Mom knew I knew it. If I'd stayed quiet maybe she would have kept smiling; maybe, since I'd finally done something Ginny hadn't, she would have started noticing me for myself. Maybe she would have said she loved me.

"I'm sorry," I said, even though it didn't matter because the entire mess was one big lie. I hadn't gotten my period at all. "Mom, that was mean. I'm sorry."

"Never mind," she said, and bent to pick up the bloody sheets. She shuddered as she touched them, and for a moment I saw the room as she did, filled with garbage: heaps of wrinkled clothing, my motley collection of comics and Nancy Drew books, a stained, lumpy stuffed horse Aunt Diane had given me years ago. There was nothing beautiful in this room, nothing tragic or aesthetic or remotely old-fashioned. I'd rebelled against Mom's beloved William Morris wallpaper by painting the walls shocking pink, and the only significant decorations were Superwoman posters.

I did have one pretty thing, a Sierra Club calendar my friend Jane had given me, but I kept it on the inside of the closet door so Mom wouldn't know how much I liked it. It struck me that of all the rooms in the house, this was the one least suited to ghosts. Why wouldn't Mom let anyone into Ginny's room? Because it was haunted? But surely she'd have welcomed Ginny's ghost.

"Come on," Mom said, grasping the sheets as if they were alive and dangerous. "I'll show you how to clean these. You have to rinse them out in cold water before you put them in the wash, because hot water will bake in the blood and then the stains will never come out. I'll give you some pads; they're easier to use than tampons at first."

I followed her back into the bathroom and watched the pink water run down the drain as she rinsed out the sheets. "It's important to bathe carefully while you're menstruating," Mom said over the running water, "so you won't smell." She said it like she was explaining the difference between a verb and a noun, but on the word *smell* her nose wrinkled, and I knew she thought I already did. "And make sure you eat a good breakfast, because you may be more tired than usual. You'll need more iron."

"I know," I said. I'd learned all this in health class, along with the obligatory odds and ends about birth control and VD. Having Babies. Not Having Babies. Fifteen Fun Things To Do With A Transparent Plastic Pelvis. Nobody told you what to do about breathing at dawn, or what it meant if you started imagining ghosts.

"You'd better mark it on your calendar," my mother said, wringing out the wet sheets. "It's good to get in the habit, even though you probably won't get it every month at first."

I had a vivid vision of writing "Blood from the breathing and Ginny on the ceiling" in the little square for April 5 on the inside of my closet door, right under the picture of some flowered meadow in the Rockies. Yeah, sure. How would Mom react if she saw *that* when she was hanging up the clothing I left all over my room? Would she die? Would she think I was writing poetry on my calendar? Or would she just think I'd gone crazy?

It didn't matter. I couldn't write anything, because he might find it. Downstairs, the front door slammed. Good. He'd left for the hospital, then, and I wouldn't have to face him over breakfast. "Twenty-eight days," I said wearily, quoting my health teacher. "But every woman's different." I wondered just how different women were, because I had the feeling this was going to be happening more often than once a month.

◆ ◇ ◆

FOR THE time being, it was a convenient deception. The pad would soak up blood, like it was supposed to, and I could say I had cramps to explain why I was walking funny, with the added advantage that I had an excuse to get out of gym class. No getting teased about my fat thighs today; no being told how clumsy I was.

The gym teacher was a decent sort, as they went. "Poor Emma," she said with a laugh when I told her. "Welcome to the club. Here, I'll write you a pass to the nurse, okay? You can get some Tylenol or something."

The nurse, Myrna Halloran, was my friend Jane's mother and our next-door neighbor. I liked her because she was fat too, and still commanded respect from her eight athletic children, but my mother despised the entire family. Myrna's husband, the foreman of a road construction crew, had helped build the interstate that cut off one corner of the town. My mother hated Tom and the highway for the same reasons: both were large, dirty, and loud. Worse, Tom had earned enough money from building the road to build a rambling addition onto his house, which had been bigger than ours to begin with. The house now came perilously close to the borders of our property; the Hallorans' many children and pets often strayed over.

As far as my mother was concerned, it was bad enough that Tom and Myrna had been able to buy into the neighborhood at all. Their expansion was nearly intolerable. Mom never quite descended to calling the Hallorans white trash, but she wasn't above criticizing Myrna for having an ungroomed husband. "She's supposed to know about antisepsis," my mother said, "and you can smell that man coming a block away."

It was true. Six feet four inches and thick everywhere, with greasy hair and a beer gut, Tom always reeked of sweat; whatever he touched grew grubby and crumpled, and he seemed unable to speak in anything softer than a bellow. His hair-trigger temper was legendary, and he'd done his best to pass it along to his children.

Once I'd ask Jane how she'd learned to fight so well. She was thin, but all of it was muscle, and she didn't seem to be afraid of anything. "Ah, some kids tried to beat me up when I was little," she said. "Bunch of boys. We were playing marbles, and they took my best one and I tried to get it back, and they started hitting on me. So I ran home to get help from my brothers, right, because they were all older and bigger than I was. But Daddy was there, and when I told him what had happened he gave me a baseball bat and said, 'If you have this you'll be big enough all by yourself.' So I went back outside and chased 'em with the bat, screaming. They ran, oh my, did they *run*! They never bothered me again."

She'd laughed when she told me that story, great belly laughs like the ones her father let out when he watched Roadrunner cartoons on Saturday mornings. "Cartoons," my mother had said with a sniff once when I mentioned it. "A bunch of foolish noise. Do you suppose he knows how to read? Myrna seems well enough educated—literate, anyhow. How can she stand being married to that man? Can't she get him to take showers?"

If Myrna nagged Tom about bathing, I'd never heard it. Instead she joked cheerfully about his dirty fingernails and wiped up the stains he left on whatever he touched. "It's good you're not a criminal," she'd told him once when I was eating dinner there, "because you'd never get away with anything. You leave fingerprints the way a skunk leaves stink, Tom."

However messy Myrna's husband may have been, her office was pristine, white and soothing. The scent of honeysuckle, wafting in through an open window, mixed pleasantly with the faint smells of bandaids and antiseptic. Myrna gave me some Tylenol and a hot water bottle and let me lie down on a padded examining table. "You coming over for dinner tonight?" she asked as she covered me with a blanket. I liked being covered, even though it was such a warm day. "I know you girls have a math test tomorrow, so I figured you'd be over to study."

"Okay," I said. Studying with Jane was a good excuse not to eat at home, and one I used as often as possible. We'd lived next door to each other for years, and I'd never had the courage to talk to her much because she had so many other friends. But this year we were in the same English class, and for our first creative writing assignment Jane had written a poem about trying to wash her dog Snarky with tomato juice after he'd rolled in a dead skunk. I'd thought it was really funny, and one day after class I'd told her so.

She'd wrinkled her nose. "Your mom didn't think so. She gave me a C! Said smelly animals weren't the right things to write poetry about, and anyway I'd messed up the rhymes someplace. Huh! I worked really hard on those rhymes."

"I know," I said, feeling miserable. Nobody was ever going to like me, the way my mother acted. "I'll bet she told you so in iambic pentameter, too, so you'd feel worse about it. You should hear her at home. She thinks nobody's written good poetry since Tennyson died."

Jane laughed. "Well, she could talk all she wanted in iam—whatever you said, and I'd never know it. Who's Tennyson?"

"Some old poet," I said, feeling more miserable. Now she'd think I was showing off. "He lived in England a long time ago and wrote a bunch of poems about King Arthur and people who died. My mother thinks he's God. She doesn't like my poetry, either."

"Really?" Jane said. She sounded surprised. "She didn't like that one about the Munsters dressing up as the Brady Bunch for Halloween?"

"She thought it was silly."

"Who are you supposed to write like? A ninety-five-year-old nun?"

"I'm supposed to write like Tennyson. He never would have written a poem about the Munsters, even if they'd had TV back then."

"He sounds boring," said Jane. "I'll bet he didn't write about smelly dogs, either. Do you want to come to our house for dinner?"

I'd eaten with the Hallorans that night, and since then I'd gone to their house at least twice a week. I was always surprised at how warmly they welcomed me. Didn't they know my mother hated them? When Jane gave me the Sierra Club calendar for Christmas, because she knew how much I liked the lake outside town, I was almost too embarrassed to thank her. I hadn't bought her anything.

"Wait," I said, "I'll bring you something," and I ran home and got a bunch of my old Nancy Drew books, the ones I had two of because Aunt Diane had sent me some for my birthday once. Ever since then, Jane had been talking about how we'd have to have an adventure and solve a mystery. But lately she'd started spending more time with other kids, especially boys, and I was afraid she thought I was boring. What would she have said if she'd known I'd seen a ghost?

But I hadn't really seen a ghost, had I? Ghosts didn't exist. Then again, you weren't supposed to bleed until you got your period, either, and that was happening. So maybe Ginny was a real ghost, and I was having an adventure instead of going crazy. But how could I tell?

"We're having apple pie for dessert tonight," Myrna Halloran said, snapping me back into the world of hot water bottles and math tests. "And I've got some vanilla ice cream."

"Great," I said. "That will be nice."

"Do your parents mind that you eat at our house so often?"

I tensed, even lying there with the hot water bottle which was supposed to relax me. What was she really asking? Did she actually want to know what my parents thought, or was she dropping a hint that it was high time I asked Jane to have dinner at our house? Nearly everybody thought I was a snob because my father was a hot-shot doctor and my mother used fancy words; did the Hallorans think so too?

I wanted to have Jane over for dinner, but I couldn't. It was bad enough that I ate at the Hallorans' so often. Jane, if neater than her father, still stood for everything that was unacceptable about her parents. If Jane came over and my father wasn't at home, Mom would talk about poetry in a way calculated to make Jane feel stupid.

And if he was home it would be even worse, because Jane was prettier than I was. She had thick red hair and long legs, and even though she was skinny she already had bigger breasts than I did. I'd seen him watching her through the window once, and he'd smiled and said, "Your little friend's going to be a heartbreaker in a few years. Why don't you ever bring her over, Emma?"

I didn't bring her over because she was my friend, and I couldn't let her get stared at like that. And even if he didn't stare at her, I couldn't let her see him staring at me, much less let her hear the conversations they had about me: the famous doctor discussing surgical procedures for obesity, making amiable jokes about wiring my mouth shut or stapling my stomach, Mom taking my part and chiding him, only to turn around and tell me how I might look a little like lovely Jane Burden, William Morris' wife, if only I'd slim down. "Ginny was light as a bird," she'd say, and heap my plate with food.

"Emma?" said Myrna Halloran. "Are you all right?"

No. I'm not all right. "Yeah," I said. "Just cramps."

"Breathe," Myrna said, frowning. "Breathe into the pain, hon. Your breathing's shallow, and that's not helping."

She coached me on breathing for a few minutes, the way I'd heard women got coached when they had babies. "Better?" Myrna said, and I nodded, amazed. I'd always thought women breathed like that to remind themselves that there were scarier things than having kids. I hadn't believed that there were ways to breathe that made things hurt less, instead of more.

"If it's really bad your dad can prescribe something for you. It may get easier once your body's used to what's going on."

"I don't think so," I said. When Myrna's frown deepened, I realized that I should have kept my mouth shut.

"No? Why not, hon?"

I swallowed. "Don't know. Just don't think so."

She was watching me very carefully now, too carefully, as carefully as he ever did over dinner. "Emma, you don't look too good. You didn't look good when you came in here. What happened?"

"Huh? Nothing. I got my period, is all."

"You've got a bruise coming out," Myrna said matter-of-factly. "On your arm. How'd you get that?"

Blood and bruises. He hadn't been elegant at all, had he? I moved my arm under the blanket, trying to make it look casual, and said, "I don't know. Something in gym, I guess. Maybe I got hit by a softball."

"Softball was last week," Myrna said gently. "You've been doing calisthenics since Monday, and it's a new bruise."

"Look," I said, trying to keep my voice steady, "I probably just walked into furniture or something. I don't remember." I shivered then, realizing that I sounded like Ginny. "It doesn't matter. It's only a bruise."

"All right," Myrna said, but she didn't sound as if she believed me, and I hated lying to someone I liked. "Do you feel well enough to stay in school today? You can go home if you want to."

"No." He probably wouldn't be home anytime during the day, but you could never tell. "I don't want to go home. I can't miss the review session for that math test tomorrow."

"All right, Emma. But come back if you change your mind. Do you think you'll still be at our house for dinner tonight?"

"Yes," I said. I'd suddenly realized how I could offer Jane an adventure and find out whether Ginny had been real, all at the same time.

The rest of the day passed in a blur. At one point I saw Myrna talking to my mother in the hall, and my stomach clenched; but when I stopped by Mom's classroom after lunch she gave me one of her sweet public smiles, a little more guarded than usual, and said only, "Myrna Halloran told me you got cramps after all. Are you all right now?"

"Yes," I told her. "I'm going to Jane's house after school so we can study for the math test."

The smile vanished at once. "Emma, how in heaven's name can you study anything there? The place is always full of screaming children, and they must keep the television on twenty-four hours a day. Soap operas and game shows, stupid celebrities chattering trifles: just what you need to prepare for an exam."

The Hallorans' TV alternated between sports and PBS, and the loudest person in the house was Tom, but there was no point in saying so. Mom must have had cramps herself, because she'd never been this bitchy about the Hallorans where someone from the outside world might hear her. They were much more popular at school than she was.

She tugged at a stray wisp of hair, and for a moment she looked so much like Ginny that it gave me goosebumps. "I don't see why you won't let your father help you with homework. Your grades would probably be better."

I'd made honor roll four marking periods in a row. No sense saying that, either; Mom would just remind me that it hadn't been high honor roll. "When, Mom? He's always at the hospital." Except at dawn. "Jane's good at math."

"Well, bring her over to our house where it's quiet, then. Do you really have to go over there all the time?"

This time I will be bringing her over, I thought, but you're so deaf you'll never know about it. "I already told her mother I'd be eating with them," I said. "I might as well go straight there."

She turned her head away from me, and I saw her throat quivering. "Pizza," she said. "Pizza and potato chips.

That's what they live on, isn't it? On that diet you'll get as big as their house."

"Oh, come on, Mom. Give them a break. They grow their own salad, you know. I can't eat your flowers, can I?"

"If the state of my rose bushes is any indication, their dogs are doing vile things to the lettuce. *I* wouldn't eat their salad."

"They haven't asked you to," I said, and watched her face turn white. I was really asking for it: she might say I couldn't go there at all. I swallowed and said, "Mom, they wash everything before they eat it. Mrs. Halloran's a nurse; she's not going to give her kids the plague. She cares about nutrition as much as you do, really she does. Don't worry."

"I won't," she said coldly, and went back to grading vocabulary quizzes.

♦ ◇ ♦

As I'd expected, I didn't have much trouble convincing Jane to go to the lake instead of home. "It's too nice a day to stay inside," I told her. "We can study after dinner."

"Sure," she said. "You're the one who's always so hyped on studying. We can go to the beach and get some sun—"

"Not the beach," I said. "Another place."

"Huh? Where?"

"A place I know," I said. "Where we can talk without anybody hearing us. I have to tell you a secret. It's about an adventure."

Jane shook her head. "You're talking like a book."

My eyes stung. "Aw. Come on, Jane. I thought you liked adventures."

"Well, sure, if it's fun. Will it be fun?"

"Sure," I said.

"This had better be good, Emma."

"It will. I promise."

So I took her to my favorite spot at the lake. A mile north of town, and accessible only by dirt roads, the lake was the only place where I was always happy. I loved it even in the summer, when everybody went swimming. I hated wearing a bathing suit, because it showed too much of my body, but once I was in the water people couldn't see me. I was safe in the water; I could stay there for hours.

Sometimes I thought I should have been born as a whale or a walrus, some big animal that was graceful underwater, even though it had a lot of fat. It was good to be fat in the water. Fat helped you float, and it kept you warm. "You have your very own wetsuit," my father had told me when he was teaching me to swim. He'd smiled when he said it, and he'd even complimented me on my endurance. I knew he wanted me to swim a lot so I'd lose weight, but I liked the compliment anyway. Today I clung to that memory, because so many others were spoiled.

It wasn't warm enough to go in the water yet, even if I did have my own wetsuit, but that meant I could wear jeans and a sweatshirt and not have to worry about anybody seeing too much of me. And the lake was beautiful: silver water surrounded by tall green trees. You saw deer come out of the woods to drink sometimes, when there weren't too many people around, and there were always birds and frogs and waterbugs. Schools of minnows swam in the shallows, casting intricate shadows on the bottom; the water reflected shifting patterns of leaves and clouds. There was always something to watch.

Jane usually went to the eastern beach, where the other kids hung out and blasted their radios, but today I took her to a small abandoned dock on the western shore, where you could almost forget that anybody else was around. I spent hours there, safe in the knowledge that no one could find me. I'd never told anyone about the dock before.

"Aren't you hot in that shirt?" she said as we walked there. We were both sweating. "I should think you'd at least roll up the sleeves."

"I'm okay." Jane's skimpy shorts and tank top embarrassed me; I was uncomfortable even looking at her. "I don't want to get bug bites."

"So use bug spray. Shoot, Emma. You wear too much clothing. Me, I'd be dying in all that stuff. Where is this place?"

"We're almost there," I said. I hoped she'd like it.

She didn't. "This is your secret place?" she said when we got there. "This old dock? Everybody knows about this place. They don't come here 'cause the beach is more fun, that's all."

I felt myself turning red. Now Jane thought I was a fool. Did people know I'd been coming here? Had they been watching me? "It's just a place to talk," I said. "It's not the secret."

"Okay, so quit being so weird and tell me the secret."

"You have to promise not to tell anybody."

"I can't do that until I know what it is."

"Jane!"

"I'll promise if it's something that won't hurt anybody."

"Of course it won't hurt anybody! I wouldn't do that."

"Okay. So tell."

"All right." This wasn't going very well, and I was getting nervous. I drummed my hand on the wooden dock and got a splinter. Great. "Okay. There's this locked room in my house, see—"

"What's in it?"

"I don't know what's in it. It's locked."

"Why's it locked?"

"My mom doesn't want anybody in there."

"Oh. Like my mom and her study. You can't go in there when your mom's in there? It's her quiet place? Is that it?"

Every room was my mother's quiet place. "No, she doesn't go in there. Nobody goes in there. That's why I need your help, because I want to find out what's in the room." If I could get into Ginny's room, maybe I could find proof that she was real. The bracelet she'd talked about, or those yellow pajamas. Then I'd know I wasn't going crazy. But I couldn't tell Jane about Ginny, because then she'd really think I was weird.

"If your mom doesn't want you in there she must

have a reason," Jane said. "Anyway, what am I supposed to do about it?"

"Well, see, I can't find the key—"

"Try the key to another room, maybe. I can't pick locks, Emma."

"The other rooms don't have locks. Not working ones, anyway. My mother had this one put on before I was born."

"Wow," Jane said, and laughed. "She really doesn't want you in there." But at least she sounded interested now. "What do you think you're going to find, anyhow? A dead body or something?"

My mouth got dry. "I don't know. But it must be something pretty interesting. So anyhow, you know that big ladder your dad used when he was painting your house? Do you still have it?"

Jane started giggling. "Shoot, Emma! What, we're going to drag that ladder out of the garage and climb into this room and nobody will see us? Are you crazy? That ladder must weigh about thirty thousand pounds, anyhow. We couldn't even carry it. Use your own ladder."

"We don't have one," I said. "My father hires people with equipment for stuff like that—"

"Oh, people like us, right? Because he's too busy being a rich doctor and having dinner with the mayor? Huh! Can't even get his hands dirty with paint."

"He gets his hands dirty all the time," I said, my throat constricting. "He cuts people open."

Jane glared at me. "He hardly even says hello to any of us."

"Well, I do, don't I? Come on, Jane, you have to help me—"

"No, I don't," she said. "The whole thing's nuts. If your mom doesn't want you in there you shouldn't go in there. You're asking me to steal my dad's ladder—"

"Not steal! Just borrow!"

"It's wrong," Jane said. "If Daddy caught us he'd be mad. It's dangerous; we might fall. Anyhow, we wouldn't get away with it, even if we did it at night. Even if we got the ladder out of the garage without my folks knowing about it, you think we're going to climb into that room without anybody noticing?"

"We could do it when my dad was at the hospital," I said. "My mother never hears a thing."

"Your *mother*? Are you kidding? Emma, you even *think* about whispering to somebody in that class and she's on you like fur on a gorilla. Forget it. This whole thing's stupid."

"But—"

"I don't want to talk about it anymore. Hey, look. Here come Tad and Billy. I wonder what they're doing all the way over here?"

She finally sounded happy, but my stomach clenched. We were out here alone, miles from the beach, and boys were coming. Big boys, bigger than we were. They were both wrestlers; they won prizes for keeping people pinned on mats. "We'd better leave," I said. "Do they see us?"

"What? Of course they see us, dodo! They're coming to say hello. What's your problem?"

"Nothing," I said, although I felt as if I were about to be sick. I didn't see how Jane could be so comfortable around boys. It must have been because she had all those brothers. "I don't like them, that's all."

"Huh. Well, *I* think Billy's cute, personally. Hey, Billy!"

Billy sat behind me in social studies, and I thought he was a dumb hulk. But she was calling him and waving, and we were on the dock, on a thin piece of wood sticking out into the water. They could stand at the end of it and keep us from getting back into shore; they could throw us down and pin us and no one would know because we were so far from the beach.

I never should have brought Jane here. I was safe here by myself, but she attracted too much attention, and now everyone would know where I went when I wanted to be alone. I needed a place to be safe, and she'd ruined it. But I'd never been safe, had I? Everyone had known about the dock all along. I hadn't been safe at all.

"How you doing?" Billy asked, slouching towards us. His fingers were as big around as sausages.

Tad trailed behind him, looking hot and bored and stupid. "Hey, Jane. Emma. Just hanging out? I thought you geniuses studied all the time."

"Nah," Jane said. "Too nice a day." She started talking to Billy about the math test while Tad stared at her breasts beneath the thin cotton. Nobody was paying any attention to me.

They'd seen us here and knew we were alone, and Billy was distracting her while Tad stared at her, just stared, stared all he wanted and thought about what he wanted to do to her. I could see the gleam in his eyes, see him wiping his palms on his jeans.

How could she keep talking about math? Couldn't she tell what was happening? She wasn't even paying attention, just sitting there chattering at Billy. He started boasting about the latest wrestling meet, and Tad took a step closer to Jane.

"There's an old rowboat around here someplace," he said, interrupting Billy's description of his winning hold. "Somebody just left it on shore. We were going to look for it and see if it would float and go out in it. Want to come?"

"Sure," Jane said. She stood up, and her breasts jiggled, and Tad wiped his hands on his jeans again. "Does it have oars? You mean somebody just left it there?"

"It'll be an adventure," Billy said cheerfully, and I hated him because he was using my word. Had he and Tad heard me talking to Jane about Ginny's room? Had they been spying on us? "If it sinks, we can all swim back to shore."

The boat wasn't hers any more than the ladder was. It didn't even belong to her family. How could she do this? "It's not yours," I said, too loudly, thinking of how much more Jane's tank top would show if it were wet. I knew I should warn her, but my throat wouldn't form the words. You mustn't ever tell anyone, he'd said, and I couldn't. "You shouldn't take it if it isn't yours. Right, Jane?"

They all looked at me as if they'd forgotten I was there, and Billy laughed. "Oh, come on, Emma. Whoever had it, they don't want it anymore, or they wouldn't have left it there. They abandoned it."

"It's not safe," I said, looking straight at Jane. There

were two of them. She didn't have her baseball bat with her, and I'd be no help at all. I'd never been any good at fighting. "The boat's not ours and we have to go study. We shouldn't have come here anyway."

"It was your idea," said Jane. She looked a lot like her mother when she frowned. "I think the boat sounds like fun. We can put it in the water, anyway, see what happens—"

"I want to study," I said. "I'm not as good at math as you are. I'll fail the test."

Tad was scowling, but Billy just laughed. "What the fuck, Emma, you'd get straight A's if you didn't open a book all year. You didn't come out here to do algebra, did you?"

"She's just scared she'll sink the boat," said Tad. "She must weigh double what I do."

I felt myself turning red. Jane made a face at Tad, and Billy said, "If she does, it's 'cause she's got twice as much brains and manners."

Jane grinned. "Tad, you're a jerk. Emma, don't mind him. You go back home and study, and I'll go with them. That's easy, isn't it?"

What was she saying? There were two of them. She'd be outnumbered. "You have to help me," I said. I remembered the round balloons with their little stubby legs. That was what I looked like; even Jane probably laughed at me behind my back.

I couldn't stand the idea of Jane making fun of me, so I thought about the swimming lessons. "Don't let the racers intimidate you," my father had said. "You're not fast, but you're steady."

I had endurance, and I had to keep her from going

out in the boat. I took a breath and said, "Please, Jane. You said you'd help me."

"No, I didn't," she said, and I knew she was talking about the ladder. A breeze had sprung up and her nipples showed under the tank top, and Tad stared at her chest even harder than he had before.

"I don't feel well," I said. My own nipples hurt just watching him look at her. "I want to go back to your house and study now so I can go to bed early. The sun's not even out anymore."

"It went behind a cloud," Billy said. "A little cloud, Emma, see? Here it comes again. Shazam!" He gestured dramatically at the sky just as the sun reappeared, and Jane giggled. "See, I'm a magician."

Go back in, I prayed to the sun. Go back behind a cloud. Catch up to the sun, cloud, and cover it the way Jane should cover her breasts, the way we should all cover ourselves so no one stares at us.

The sky didn't listen to me, any more than Jane was listening. "Just for an hour," she told Billy and Tad, "and then I really have to go home and study. You don't have to come if you don't want to, Emma. I'll help you with math after dinner. You're still coming over for dinner, right?"

"Yes," I said, defeated. But where was I going to go until then? The dock wasn't safe any more, and if I went home Mom would find some way to keep me from going to the Hallorans' to eat. I could go the library and study, but I knew it wouldn't work. I hated math; I'd just sit there feeling miserable because I was fat. Or else I'd keep thinking about Ginny and worrying about whether I was crazy.

◆

I had to find out. Mom wasn't expecting me home; she wouldn't hear me if I snuck into the house. I'd creep around and look for the key some more. I'd pretend I was Nancy Drew.

The plot didn't make me happy, though, because I'd be doing it by myself and we lived in a big house. I knew I could search for years, dig up all the floorboards and sift though every bit of dust in the attic, and still never find the key. To give myself time to think of new places I took the long way home through the woods, or what was left of them after the ravages of the highway Tom Halloran had helped build, but that didn't work either. I kept hearing highway noises through the trees and imagining truckers pulling over to the side of the road, crashing through the underbrush to find me; with each flicker of sunlight on leaves, I seemed to see Ginny flitting through the branches, mocking me with her beauty.

The route would have taken me to our back door, but before I reached my house I had to pass the Hallorans', and there was Myrna in her tomato bed, pulling up weeds. Snarky, Snotty, Slimy, and Spot, tethered to chains from which they inevitably escaped, set up a four-part mongrel chorus when they saw me. No one else was in the backyard.

"Emma!" Myrna said, looking up from her tomatoes. "There you are. I thought you and Jane would be upstairs with your noses in the books. Where is she?"

"With Billy and Tad," I said. "In a rowboat on the lake."

"Sounds like fun. Why didn't you go with them?"

"I didn't feel like it. I have to study."

"Those are good reasons," Myrna said cheerfully.

"How *do* you feel? You look a little better than you did this morning."

I shrugged. "I'm okay."

"Are you?" She stood up, dusting earth and bits of grass from her slacks. "Come inside and let me look at that bruise, and then I'll give you some lemonade."

"I'm fine," I said. "I'm going home now. You don't need to look at my arm."

"No?" She raised one eyebrow. "Well, all right. Would you like the lemonade anyway?"

I reddened again. Myrna was being nice to me because she knew I didn't feel well, and I was being rude back. I didn't need Mom to tell me that Ginny never would have behaved so badly. "Yes, please."

"Good," she said, leading me inside. The house was unusually quiet now that the canine opera in the backyard had faded to whimpers. I couldn't hear anyone talking; the TV wasn't even on.

"Where is everybody?"

Myrna laughed. "Tom's working and there are no kids here—can you believe it? Jane's on the lake and Mike and Andrew are at track practice, and Rob's over at the Smiths', and Greg's playing touch football with some of the Wilson boys and David's at a play rehearsal. And John and Tom Jr. are busy with their own families and haven't even spared me any grandchildren to spoil. You've never seen this place so empty, have you?"

"No," I said. During the time she'd been talking, three of the Hallorans' five cats had wound themselves around my ankles, and the four dogs had resumed their commotion. They clearly weren't used to the quiet either, since there were usually at least two children of various ages—not to mention nieces, nephews and hangers-on—to lavish them with affection. My mother called the Halloran household a rabbit warren, but Myrna's philosophy was simple. "There's always room for one more," she'd say, and set another place at the table.

As a result, the Hallorans' kitchen always looked like a bomb had exploded somewhere: the dishwasher remained perpetually open and half full, and piles of dishes—both dirty and clean—dotted the counter. The refrigerator was papered with layers of cartoons, grocery lists, first-grade art, recipes, and newspaper articles about health tips, local elections, and gardening. The strata of clippings probably went back ten years; I often wondered how long it had been since the actual surface of the refrigerator had been visible. Next to the telephone hung a huge bulletin board similarly festooned; the only piece of paper not partially obscured by ten other pieces of paper was a large list, carefully lettered in bright red marker readable halfway across the room, of emergency numbers. With the Hallorans' usual excess, the list extended beyond the standard trio of police, fire, and ambulance to include the Animal Hospital, the Poison Control Center, and the National Guard.

My mother hated the Hallorans' kitchen. I found it comforting. Myrna plucked a glass from one of the clusters on the counter—I trusted her to know that it was clean—and poured a glass of lemonade from a huge Tupperware jug. "Here you go, hon. Any idea when Janie'll be back?"

"She said an hour."

Myrna laughed. "Maybe by dinner, then. Whose boat was it?"

I hesitated, unwilling to tell on Jane. Myrna's undivided attention was making me claustrophobic. I bent down and patted one of the cats so I wouldn't have to look at her. "I don't know. I wasn't listening."

"Cramps again?"

"Yeah. But they're better now." Even if I'd been able to talk about Tad staring at Jane's breasts, I wouldn't have been able to tell Myrna I was worried because a boy was paying attention to her daughter. It would sound like I was accusing Jane of not noticing, of being stupid or foolish.

But Jane herself entered the kitchen at that moment, soaking wet, the thin cotton tank top plastered to her breasts just as I had feared it would be. They must have grabbed her in the boat; she must have had to dive overboard to get away from them. No one could swim as fast as Jane could. She was lucky she could swim so fast.

"What happened?" Myrna asked, both eyebrows raised.

"Tad tried to touch me," Jane said cheerfully, grabbing a towel from the laundry hamper sitting in the middle of the kitchen table, "so I punched him and he fell into the water, and it turned out he couldn't *swim*—can you believe that, I mean, he takes this old boat out when we aren't even sure it will float and he can't swim, is that dumb or what?—so I had to go in after him so the idiot wouldn't drown. And him bigger than me and everything! Boy, was he ever embarrassed. Trying to feel me up and then I saved his life. Billy thought the whole thing was hilarious. He was laughing so hard he could hardly row the boat."

My stomach was a lump of ice. Now we'd really get it, especially since there was no one else around to provide distractions. What were you doing in a leaky boat? Why were you wearing that clothing alone with two boys? What right did you have to punch him when you'd excited him by wearing that clothing? Emma, why didn't you tell me Jane was going out in a leaky boat? Why didn't you make Jane come home instead of going out on the lake? Why didn't you give her your sweatshirt to wear over the tank top, if she was going to be alone in a leaky boat with two boys?

"Are you all right?" Myrna said.

"Huh? Are you kidding? Of course I'm all right!"

"Well, that's good." Myrna sounded like she was trying very hard not to laugh. "Is Tad all right?"

"Oh, he's fine, thanks to me." Jane shook her head, showering the kitchen with lake water. "He was more scared than anything else. And embarrassed because he'd tried to grab my boobs—"

"Jane!"

"Oh, breasts, all right, anatomically correct hoo-has, anyway, he did it once like it was a joke and I yelled at him and Billy said he'd better not do it again, but Tad said girls were supposed to like that and tried to do it again anyway, so I punched him. I think I may have knocked one of his teeth loose."

"How did you feel when he did that?" Myrna said.

"Huh? Mad!"

"Good. Tell me what you would have done if you'd

been alone on the beach, and a grown man had tried to do that to you."

A grown man. What if it's a grown man and he's in your bedroom and he's breathing on you? You don't do anything. You lie there and wait for it to stop, because if you do anything else he'll wire your mouth shut and put staples in your stomach. He can do anything he wants to, because if you try to tell anyone your mother will die.

But Jane just said, "Oh, *Mom,*" the way she complained about being told to eat her spinach, and recited, "I'd scream as loud as I could and go for the crotch and the eyes, and when I broke away from him I'd run like hell, and if I couldn't break away or it was too dangerous to try, like he had a gun or something, I'd outthink him until I could."

How could I outthink somebody who'd gone to medical school? Where would I even start? But Myrna just nodded and said, "Good. Emma, do you know all of this?"

"All of what?" I asked, my throat very dry.

"Self-defense techniques."

Self-defense techniques. You've got to be kidding. "Yes," I said. Sure, I know how to defend myself. You keep your mouth shut and pretend to be somewhere else, because if you say anything he'll hurt you more than he's going to already, and if Mom finds out—

I could no more knee him in the groin than I could fly to the moon. That would only make it worse. Myrna didn't understand anything.

"Show me," she said crisply.

"What?"

She reached into the forest of coats and sweaters

growing on hooks from the back door and deftly extricated a thick down vest. "Show me," she repeated, putting it on. "I'm going to try to grab you and I want you to fight me off. I know how to block blows, so don't worry about hurting me, all right? I taught Janie this way. Hit as hard as you can."

I couldn't hit at all. "Can't I just scream?" I asked.

"It's good if you can scream," Myrna said, nodding approvingly. She seemed to think it had been a serious question. "A lot of women can't; they just freeze. But pretend you've screamed and it hasn't worked. Show me what you'd do then."

Jane was perched on a clear spot on the counter, eating an apple she'd found somewhere. "She's ticklish," she said, grinning. "That's what the vest is supposed to protect her from. You have to go for the back of the knees—"

"Janie! Don't tell her these things." Myrna was coming towards me, laughing, bundled in the thick vest and raising one thick arm. "Now turn around, okay, pretend you're just walking—"

"No!" I couldn't breathe. "Don't touch me! You're making this into a game and it's not funny—"

"No," Myrna said, not smiling any more. "No, it isn't funny at all, and I wasn't trying to make it a game. I'm sorry I upset you. Emma, what's wrong?"

She knew too much. I was telling her too much; she was going to find out. I swallowed, fighting for air, and said, "Why don't you ask her about the boat? They stole somebody's boat and they didn't even know what kind of shape it was in. And Tad—he was—he was *looking*! If she'd had her eyes open she'd have known! If she hadn't been wearing that shirt—"

I stopped, appalled. What had I said? How could I have said that? Jane, white-faced, slid off the counter in one quick movement and darted toward me, her fists clenched, but Myrna put an arm around her shoulders and held her. "Janie, be still. Emma, I was going to ask about the boat later. I was. The boat's important, but what Tad did is more important, and what Jane did to defend herself is even more important than that. Do you understand? Emma, please tell me what's wrong."

"I have to leave now," I said. Jane hated me. I could tell from the way she looked at me, her face perfectly still and her jaw clenched: she'd beat me into a pulp if Myrna weren't holding her, and she'd be right to do it. I'd made her promise not to tell about the ladder, and then I'd gone and told about the boat. I was slimier than Snarky's dead skunk.

"Wait," Myrna said. "Emma, it's a great gift to realize when you're in danger. It's an even greater gift to be able to get yourself out of it. We all need to know how to do both of those things. Do you understand?"

"Yes," I said, and ran out of the kitchen. There was no way I could get myself out of it. He'd outthought me a long time ago.

On my way out I collided with Tom. He'd been coming in the front door and I hadn't even seen him, because I was so desperate to get out of the house that I hadn't been looking at what was in front of me. He was wearing smelly work clothing, and when I ran into his stomach he grabbed my shoulders and said in his characteristic near-bellow, "Whoa. Whoa there, little Emma! What's the hurry?"

"I'm late for dinner," I said, and wrenched myself away from him. I couldn't stand anything about him: his hands or his stink or the way you could hear his heavy breathing under each syllable whenever he spoke. How could Jane and Myrna stand to listen to him breathing like that?

"Careful," he told me, laughing, and moved aside to let me pass. I skittered across the porch and down the steps, and tripped and fell spectacularly onto the Hallorans' front walk. My palms and one knee took all my weight, and I lay collapsed on all fours for a moment, stunned and helpless. Tom Halloran would see me lying here and come pick me up, and I wouldn't be able to run away from him because I couldn't even stand—

But he had evidently already gone into the kitchen, because I heard his voice from the back of the house. "Karate lessons again, Myrna? Jane, you're wet. And why did Emma Gray just go streaking out of here like a bat out of hell?"

Myrna murmured something I couldn't make out, and then Jane's voice rose, wounded and angry. "If you'd heard what she *said*—"

"What?" Tom's voice was sharper now. "She insulted you? What?"

Myrna was murmuring again and I was on my feet, somehow, my hands scraped raw and my knee oozing blood through torn denim. I half-ran, half-limped the few feet home, afraid I'd hear Jane in pursuit at any moment. My father's car wasn't in the driveway; he was still at the hospital, then, and I wouldn't have to explain why I looked this way. Good.

But Mom was home, sitting at our huge polished wooden dining room table. In front of her were two lit candles, a bud vase with a single white rose in it, and a sheet of paper. She'd taken her hair down, and it shone reddish gold in the candlelight. She jumped when I came in, and stared as if I were the ghost, and swept the paper into her lap. Poetry, no doubt. The stuff she wrote to Ginny. I'd found some of it once when I'd been looking for the key, but for all the hours Mom spent on it, she wasn't giving Tennyson much competition. Lots of angels and flowers, and Ginny a bland simpering presence amongst them. Even if I only wrote poetry about dumb TV shows, I knew that Mom's stuff was fifth-rate Hallmark card.

"Sorry," I said, breathless. "Did I interrupt your seance?" She was eating cottage cheese and honeydew melon from our best china, and her fork was part of the solid sterling set that had been her mother's. She ate by candlelight whenever she could, but she must have been feeling really snooty about the Hallorans' vegetables, if she couldn't even use normal plates. "I didn't mean to break the mood, Mom."

"Don't be ridiculous," she said, standing up and snapping her napkin. She clutched the piece of paper in her other hand. "I wasn't expecting you home, that's all." She took a step closer, peering at me in the flickering light, and said, "My god, Emma—what have you done to yourself?"

"I fell on the Hallorans' steps."

I was expecting a lecture about how Ginny never would have been clumsy enough to fall down a few steps, but instead she said, "Well, that's hardly a surprise. Their property's a gigantic obstacle course. Myrna Halloran didn't even offer to clean you up? She's a nurse, isn't she?"

"She didn't know I fell," I said. "I was leaving their house. I came straight home." Aren't you going to offer to clean me up? You're my mother, aren't you?

She sighed. "You're certainly a mess. Go into the bathroom and scrub those scrapes out with peroxide. You didn't break anything, did you?"

If Jane had come home bleeding, Myrna would have cleaned the wound herself, as gently and quickly as possible because she knew it hurt. She cleaned everyone's cuts that way. But I couldn't go to Myrna, because I'd tattled on Jane.

"No," I said, and limped into the bathroom. I was gingerly dabbing at the deepest scrape with a washcloth when I heard the front door slam. He was home. I started working faster, too fast, scrubbing even though it made me wince and cry, because the last thing in the world I wanted was for him to do it.

"What a nice surprise," Mom said, her voice suddenly high and girlish. "Everyone's back early tonight. I thought you had emergency surgery?"

"The appendix ruptured. The internal medicine people waited too long to make their diagnosis, as usual. We can't operate until the patient stabilizes. Emma's here too, I take it?"

I opened the bathroom door and walked out into the hallway. "Hi," I said. "I fell, but I cleaned the cuts. I have a math test tomorrow and I have to study, so I'm going to the library—"

"You're going to eat dinner first, young lady. Especially since your father's home. You don't get to see him very often."

That's because I don't look. I wish I couldn't hear him, either. "Don't I get a hug?" he asked.

You get too many. But I gave him one of those quick, wooden embraces reserved for people you have to be nice to, and he laughed. "That's a little better. How'd you hurt yourself?"

Don't you remember? It was only this morning. "I told you: I fell."

"She tripped down the Hallorans' steps," my mother called from the kitchen. "They probably had a loose board or a nail sticking up or something. Maybe you should give her a tetanus shot."

He'd be delighted if I got tetanus. Then I'd have lockjaw and couldn't tell anybody anything, and I'd lose weight the way he wanted me to. And I'd die, like Ginny. Maybe then Mom would love me.

He'd seated himself in one of the dining room chairs, where he sprawled, langorous and handsome in the candlelight, as sleek and long-boned as one of those men you see in ads for expensive cars. "Mmmmph," he said, pretending to listen to Mom, but he was watching me, staring at me the way Tad had stared at Jane. Even if he stopped breathing in my bedroom, even if he never made me bleed again, I'd never be able to get away from his eyes.

"And she's a nurse," my mother complained, with a vigorous rattle of saucepans. "Living in that filth—"

I found my voice for a moment, hoping conversation

would make him stop looking at me. "It's not filth, Mom. It's just mess."

My mother snorted. "I'm sure you feel completely at home there, Emma, the way you keep your room."

He still watched me with a faint smile, absentmindedly rubbing one thigh exactly the way Tad had. I started to shake, and the smile deepened. "Well," he said, "Myrna can't be very serious about nursing, or she'd be working at the hospital, instead of babysitting children with runny noses and scraped elbows."

"That doesn't make sense," I said hoarsely. "That's like saying that no one who knew anything about poetry would teach junior-high English instead of high school or college."

Come on, Mom. Start talking about the importance of education. Help me distract him. Please . . . but I wasn't even sure she'd heard me in the clatter of dishes, and my father only looked amused. "That's not a bad point, Emma."

Trapped. Trapped. I'd been disagreeing with him, but he was going to make it look like I'd been insulting Mom's intelligence.

"Yes it is," I said. "It's wrong. You have to teach kids things when they're young—"

He threw his head back and laughed soundlessly, shaking with mirth but doing it so discreetly that Mom would never hear it from the kitchen, any more than she heard the predawn gasping in my bedroom. "Literature," I said, shaking in earnest now. "Nutrition and stuff. That's what I was talking about—"

"Nutrition," Mom said proudly, carrying a steaming platter into the dining room, and I remembered our conversation that morning, several lifetimes ago. She was congratulating herself on how well she fed me again. "A good hearty pot roast; I thought I'd have to save it for Sunday dinner, but since everyone's home—"

She was cut short by a bellow from next door.

"No," Tom Halloran said, projecting as clearly as if he were speaking through a bullhorn, "No, Janie's not going to apologize and I'm bloody damn well not paying your dental bills! Now get the hell off my porch!"

"Heavens," my father said, raising both eyebrows. "What's all this about?"

"Whatever it is," Mom said, "it sounds too good to miss." She put down the roast and blew out the candles so that the room was completely dark, and then moved to the window and pulled aside the Morris-patterned drapes. I reluctantly moved to stand next to her, unwilling to be alone in any unlighted room with my father. Edward Ewmet, even less appetizing than his son—would Tad be that hunched and bald when he was older?—stood wringing his hands on the Hallorans' front steps. His melodious voice, the pride of the local Lutheran church where he was a deacon, was too soft to understand, but the tone managed to be both obsequious and condescending.

"Oooh," my mother said, "Oh, he's just like Uriah Heep, isn't he? Look at him!"

"And Tom Halloran's like Falstaff," my father answered. He'd come up behind us; his hand brushed the back of my neck, and I jerked away from him as if I'd been shot. "He's going to have a real beaut of a coronary one of these days. I hope Myrna's taken out a good life insurance policy on him."

Another melodious murmur from Ewmet wafted across the lawn, interrupted by an even louder bellow from Tom. "Now look here, man: if you'd done that you'd be called a child molester and thrown in jail and butt-fucked by a bunch of jailbirds—and probably get your jewels sliced off and stuffed in your ears, 'cause they don't like child molesters either! If you can't teach your kid not to do things that'll get him thrown in jail when he grows up it's your own damn problem. Don't expect me to feel sorry for him."

"Emma," my mother said, "what's been going on over there?"

"I don't know."

"Really? Jane doesn't tell you about her little adventures? I thought you were with her after school?"

"I told you, I don't know anything."

My father had started his soundless laughter again. His hand, as persistent as the mosquito you never manage to kill, the one whose whine drones through all your summer nightmares, casually brushed my back. I leaned forward as if to hear better, trying to get away from him, wondering if he could smell my sweat and the stink of blood underneath it. Yes, of course he could. He'd described the smell of the operating room once, the sharp scent of disinfectant mixing with the metallic tang of blood, the reek of cauterized flesh.

"The same *age*?" roared Tom Halloran. "They're the same age, and that's supposed to excuse it? Oh, that's a good one. So he's only going to molest women his own age when he grows up: real model citizen you're raising here, you know that?"

Ewmet's words, raised from murmur to whine, became audible now. "But he's only a child! He didn't know any better!"

"So's Janie only a child," said Tom Halloran, "and she taught him better, didn't she? For that matter, she bloody well saved his life, which is a good sight more than I'd have done in her position. While you're teaching your boy not to molest the ladies, you'd better teach him to swim."

Ewmet, as red-faced and spluttering as if he'd just been hauled out of the lake himself, said, "Well, sir, I didn't want to say this, but if you send your girl out in this warm weather without a bra—"

"Oh?" answered Tom Halloran, rising on his toes. "Oh, excuse me, and if I do that—what does it mean, *sir*? That the neighborhood is thereby invited to grope her howsomuchever they desire?"

"One can't blame the boys for presuming—"

"Yes," Tom Halloran said, "one can. One can blame *your* boy for being a rude little shit. Billy Washoe didn't try to grope Janie, and he's the same age your Tad is! What you can't do, *sir*, is blame my girl for defending herself. And you can't blame her for not wearing some asinine piece of clothing she doesn't need and doesn't like. If Janie walked outside buck naked and somebody touched her without her permission, she could knock all his teeth down his throat and I'd tell her she was right to do it! And if you give me any more bullshit, I'm going to do the same thing to you she did to your asswipe son, you bastard! Get out of here!"

Ewmet got, muttering hostilities over his shoulder. Next to me, my mother shook her head; my father, chuckling, stood behind us, an arm around each of us. "Well," he said. "That was quite a show, wasn't it?"

"What horrible people," Mom said. "That man must drink, the way he screams all the time. You were over there, Emma. Was he drunk?"

"No, Mom." This was one of my mother's pet theories about Tom Halloran, and she never listened when I told her she was wrong. "I keep telling you that. He gets drunk about as often as Dad does."

I'd never seen my father drink at all. Sometimes I wished he would, even though I knew it made other fathers mean; maybe he might have slept more. But my mother took a step backwards, as spooked as one of Aunt Diane's horses in a thunderstorm, and said, "What did you mean by that? Tell me why you said that! Who—"

"Pam! Take it easy. She didn't mean anything. She wasn't even born then, remember? She was just talking. Would you please relax?"

"What?" I said. "What are you talking about?"

"Nothing, Emma. She's not talking about anything." My father's hand brushed my hip and I shoved it away, but it came back.

Mom, oblivious, glared at me. "Something must have been happening at the Hallorans'. Why did you come home so quickly?"

"Jane was upset and wanted to talk to her mother," I said. "In private. So I left, all right?" Don't admit you know anything: don't, don't. Tattling once was bad enough. You don't even want to think about the questions he'll ask you if you admit how much you know.

She clearly didn't believe me. "Well, whatever happened, I'm sure we'll hear about it at school tomorrow."

My father snorted. "Surely you jest, dear one. It's going to be all over town within an hour, the way those two were screaming at each other. It will probably make the front page of tomorrow's paper."

"At least Jane had the good grace to be upset privately," Mom said. "Although the way her brute of a father talks, it's no surprise that she's never learned how to behave in public."

My throat tightened. "It sounded to me like Tad behaved worse than Jane did." My father's fingers were caressing the inside of my elbow now, and I was getting tired of moving away from him. That was what he counted on, always: that I'd get tired and have to go to sleep, that I'd be as still and silent as Ginny's grave when he came into my room at dawn, that I wouldn't be conscious to listen to him breathing. Because otherwise there'd be blood and disinfectant and scorched skin, and my jaw wired together or my stomach stapled.

"What?" Mom turned to look at me, her face cold, and then let the drapes fall closed. In the moment before she relit the candles, my father's finger traced the circle of one nipple in the old prompt for silence. My stomach tightened and heaved. I'd never be able to keep down Mom's pot roast tonight, no matter how much she forced on me.

"It sounds to *me* as if nothing would have happened if Jane had behaved properly," Mom said, once again lovely in the candlelight. She moved around the table, arranging gleaming silver at our three places. "She should know better than to go out half-dressed."

That's what I'd told Myrna, and Jane was going to kill me for it. I went to the sideboard and started collecting plates. Setting the table was a good excuse to get away from my father. "Yeah, well, it sounds like Tad should have known better, too. Jane doesn't take anything from anybody, and everybody knows it."

"You admire that girl entirely too much, Emma. This is the real world, remember? There's no such thing as Superwoman. What's Jane going to do—punch her way through life? This is a civilized society. You can't live that way, and her parents are doing her a terrible disservice if they tell her that she can."

"Are they?" My voice sounded strange to me, too high and far away, and I had to hold onto the plates very tightly so they wouldn't slip out of my hands. "Mr. Halloran was defending her because she's his daughter and he loves her. That's what parents are supposed to do, isn't it? Love their kids even if the kids do something wrong? Wouldn't you two have done that much for Ginny?"

I'd known better than to suggest that they'd do anything similar for me, but Mom reached me around the table in five swift steps and drew her hand back as if she were going to slap me. I raised the plates as a shield, thinking, I can't drop them. I can't drop them. She'll kill me if I drop them.

"Pamela!" My father was on his feet in an instant,

catching hold of her wrist. "Stop it! Who's acting like Jane now?"

Mom had never tried to hit me before. I couldn't imagine her hitting anybody. I'd never seen her so mad; her face was a mask of white, condensed fury. "Ginny was not a slut!" she said, her voice shaking. "Ginny was a sweet little girl!"

"Jane's not a slut either, Mom!" Her eyes narrowed, and I knew I'd said the wrong thing again. "Mom, look, that wasn't what I meant anyway, really it wasn't—"

"What did you mean, then?"

"I think what she meant," my father said sharply, putting his free arm around her waist, "is that parents are blind when it comes to their children. This is certainly true of Tom Halloran, who can't see little Jane's healthy anatomy waving in the breeze for anyone to snatch at, and unfortunately it's equally true of you where Ginny's concerned—"

Mom's face tightened. "Ginny wouldn't have—"

"Hush, love." He'd gone back to his soothing doctor voice. "No, of course she wouldn't. She devoted her existence to being every bit as pure as you demanded of her, which is why she's supping with the saints even as we speak—"

"What?" Mom had grown wild-eyed in the dancing candlelight. She tried to get away from my father, but he held her too tightly. "What are you saying? Are you blaming me that she died?"

"Oh, Pam! Of course not. I meant that she's in heaven, that's all. You're the poetic one, aren't you?"

"You think I killed her, don't you? I know you do!

You think it's my fault, because I encouraged her when we went to the circus."

The circus? I'd never been to a circus. Once when I was little I'd asked Mom about them and she'd told me they were stupid, grown people dressed in silly costumes pretending to be children. Even at the time, I'd wondered why silly costumes upset her so much.

"*You* think it's your fault," my father said calmly. "I've never blamed you, and neither has anyone else. Pam, it wasn't anybody's fault, unless you want to blame some bacteria. It just happened, and it was terrible, and we all wish we could undo it. But don't take it out on the imperfect child, all right? She's had a bad enough day, what with falling down the Hallorans' front steps. Emma, are you all right?"

"Yes."

"Did your mother hurt you?"

"No." You did. But he didn't care about that. I was a pumpkin or a balloon, something that wasn't conscious, something that just endured.

"I'm sorry," Mom said stiffly. "I shouldn't have gotten angry at you. I know you must be upset about Jane."

"Forget it."

"Honey—"

"I said forget it!" The way she said *honey* curdled my stomach. She hadn't even looked at me when she said it.

"I think," said my father, letting go of Mom's waist, "that we should eat that pot roast now."

"I can't eat," I told them. "I'm not hungry. I'm going to go up to my room and study."

"Emma! You have to eat—"

"Why? I'm fat, remember? Missing one meal won't kill me."

"Nutrition," my mother said, trying to smile.

"I don't want any dinner! I'm not hungry! I feel sick, all right? Would you leave me alone?"

"Let her go," my father said, and I fled up the stairs, favoring my sore knee. Behind me, I heard him say, "Pam, for God's sakes get rid of that thing."

What thing? I crouched at the top of the stairs and listened with ears fine-tuned by the breathing. I heard paper ripping, and he said matter-of-factly, "You've been brooding about this since last night. That's what has you so keyed up."

The poem? That had been the only paper on the table. Did he get to read Mom's poetry? Maybe he helped her with the awful rhymes. What a joke. What rhymes with life, Stewart? Knife. What rhymes with love? Shove. What rhymes with trust? Lust.

The phone rang. Maybe it would be the hospital summoning my father back to work. I crouched in the darkness of the stairwell as he said, "You'd better answer that."

"It's probably for you." Mom sounded hoarse, defeated, subdued.

"Answer the telephone," he said quietly.

Mom could assume her sweet schoolteacher voice without thinking about it, and those were the tones that came from the kitchen. "Oh, Myrna. How are you? No, Emma's fine. Just fine. And is *Jane* all right? Well, I'm certainly glad to hear *that*. No, she just skinned her knee; it's nothing serious. That's kind of you, but she's already gone upstairs to study, and I'd rather she not be interrupted. Thank you for calling."

My heart sank. The Hallorans had chewed out Tad's father and now they were looking for me. "That busybody," Mom said, and then let out a wail. "You burned it! Stewart—"

"Now, Pamela. Come on. I'm sure you had it memorized by now anyway."

"You had no right!"

"All the right in the world. It was upsetting you."

"It was also my property."

"Pamela, my love, consider it a medical procedure. A cauterized wound. The work of a few seconds that prevents possible months of pain and infection."

"I see," she said coldly. "I know but matters of the house, and you, you know a thousand things. Is that it?"

"No, that's not it. Pam, I'm sorry I upset you. Truly I am. But it's better for you to get your mind onto something else."

"It wasn't yours to burn," Mom said. She sounded hopeless again.

"What's yours is mine. Isn't that what our wedding vows said? Now look: I've already apologized for upsetting you. I don't want to discuss this any more. Do you want me to go up and look at Emma?"

No. I never should have said I wasn't feeling well. But to my infinite relief, Mom answered, "Emma's fine. She said she's studying. Let's eat our dinner. I'll take a tray up to her later, if she wants one."

There was no way in the world I'd be able to study

now, and I'd cut off any chance of getting out of the house. Even if I managed to sneak out, where could I go? The lake wasn't safe any more and neither was the Hallorans' house, and anywhere else I'd just keep picturing Ginny and wondering if I was crazy. Sleep: sleep was the only place left. Sleep would protect me at least until dawn, when nothing could.

Sleep now, then. I crawled between the clean sheets without even taking my filthy clothing off, but when I closed my eyes all I could see was the look on Jane's face when I told her mother what she'd done. I thought I'd been telling the truth, but when Tom Halloran yelled at Mr. Ewmet, he might as well have been yelling at me. Maybe he had been. Maybe he'd known that I'd be able to hear him.

But I'd been right, hadn't I? It wasn't safe to dress like that. It wasn't safe to go out in leaky boats with boys you hardly knew who were staring at you. It wasn't. It wasn't. She should have known better. She could have kept herself safe so easily: by wearing a sweatshirt and not going out in the boat, by keeping her eyes open, by using her common sense. It would have been so easy for her not to get into trouble and she'd ignored all the signals, and there was no easy way out for me at all. If wearing a sweatshirt would have stopped the breathing I'd have worn ten of them at once, but it didn't matter. He'd just wait until I fell asleep and then he'd come into my bedroom and it would start all over again, no matter how many sweatshirts I had on.

I wanted to stop thinking about it, wanted to stop thinking about everything, but sleep was impossible, and there wasn't anywhere else I could go. Or was there? Could I leave my body now, even though it wasn't dawn?

I could, and I did. The sudden absence of pain was as welcome as the first cool dive into the lake on a hot summer's day. Out of my body, I felt better than I ever had inside it.

I floated effortlessly to the ceiling and spun so it became the floor. Did I have to do that, though? Why? Why did I have to stand on anything, if I could fly? I did an experimental cartwheel—I couldn't land wrong and get hurt, since all my nerve endings were down on the bed—and discovered that it was easy. So I did a back flip and a handstand. They probably wouldn't have looked very graceful to anyone watching me, and even without a body I'd never do them as well as Ginny had, but they were a lot more fun than studying or being scared.

"Pretty good," Ginny said behind me as I was in the middle of a somersault, and if I'd been in my body I'd have fallen on my head and split my skull open.

"No, really," she said as I scrambled to turn around, "that's not bad at all, for somebody who's just starting out. You need more practice, that's all."

"What are you doing here?" She was still wearing her silly Snoopy pajamas, and when I yelled at her she picked up a piece of her hair and started chewing it. "I didn't call you! I don't want you here! You're a hallucination!"

"You didn't call me the first time, either." She looked even more real than she had before; less fuzzy around the edges, somehow, as if whatever was showing this film of her—God? my imagination?—had adjusted the focus on the projector. "And I'm as real as you are. I told you that before."

"You told me a lot of stuff. Not that any of it made any sense."

She shrugged. "Well, maybe I have to come back until it makes sense. Anyhow, here I am."

"Here you are. Why would anyone want to be *here* after being in heaven?"

She looked surprised. "I don't know. This is where I lived. I was happy here, wasn't I?"

"That's what Mom says. You were happy here, but I'm not. Want to trade places?"

She shivered and shook her head. "Can't do that. It's not my body down there; it's yours."

"Yeah, it sure is. Would you want it if you had it? It's ugly and clumsy, and right now it's got blood all over it."

Ginny looked at her feet. "You shouldn't talk like that. You did that back flip pretty well, really you did. You'd get better if you practiced."

"Sure," I said, thinking of my conversation with Jane about Tennyson. I wondered if Ginny felt as embarrassed as I'd felt then.

What was I thinking? She couldn't feel embarrassed; she couldn't feel anything, any more than balloons or pumpkins could. She was dead, and I was imagining her. But I kept talking anyway, because she'd said something nice to me. "Not having to worry about gravity helps. So you remember gymnastics now, huh?"

"Gymnastics," she said, and her face lit up the way it had when I'd said her name. "I remember a lot about gymnastics. I remember the uneven parallels: I used to get black and blue where I hit the bars, but the dismounts were like flying, and if you landed right it didn't even hurt. And I remember the balance beam. I used to pretend that it was a high wire and I was performing at the circus."

"The circus," I said, disgusted again. Here she was talking about stuff I'd just heard; she must be my imagination. "You went there with Mom, didn't you? She's never taken me."

"Yes," Ginny said, but a shadow crossed her face. "She liked it. We both liked the acrobats." She shivered then, and chewed her hair again for a minute, and then said shyly, "Do you want me to show you how to do a triple somersault?"

"No. Why should you teach me how to do that? It won't do me any good once I'm back in my fat ugly body. You might as well teach me how to fly."

"But you are flying," Ginny said. "Your mind is, anyway. And I didn't have to teach you how to do it. You figured it out by yourself, just like you did with the cartwheel."

"Great. So I'm the next incarnation of Wonder Girl, and the next time I go to the lake and somebody hassles me I can drag them up to cloud nine and dump them on top of a tree or something. You're as bad as Myrna Halloran, you know that?"

"No, I don't know her," Ginny said seriously. Her face brightened again. "I remember the lake, though. It was pretty there. I used to go sit on that old dock on the western shore when no one else was around—"

"You did? You *did*? So do I!" Idiot, I told myself, of course she does. She's you. She's your imagination. What else would she do? More suspiciously, I said, "Mom never told me you did that."

"She always thought I was at the library," Ginny said, wrinkling her nose. "I studied at the lake sometimes, but mostly I just watched the fish."

Just like me. What a surprise. "Minnows, right? The ones that make shadows on the bottom—"

"And the birds that peck in the sand looking for things to eat." She grinned, and I realized that I hadn't seen her smile before. One of her upper front teeth was chipped. Mom had never told me about that, either, and it didn't show up in any of the family photographs. Well, so I didn't want to think she was perfect. But how had I come up with the pajamas?

Ginny was still babbling about the lake. "And I used to see owls sometimes at dusk, and bats and raccoons, and once I saw a fox come to the water to drink. A big red one. It was beautiful. Have you ever seen a fox?"

"No." Just boys. "There aren't so many animals around now, I guess because there are more people or something. Just the birds and the fish, and sometimes deer. But not very often."

Ginny chewed her lip for a minute and then said, "Do you want to go there, to the lake? We can go there, if you want to."

Oh, sure we can. "Won't people see us?"

"No, silly. There won't be anybody else there. We won't *really* be there, not in the world. Just in our heads, sort of. It's hard to explain."

"You're kidding." I knew all of this was completely

crazy, but I felt the same surge of lightness as when I'd left my body. I wanted to believe in her. I did, I did. "We can go to the lake, just like that? You mean I can go to the lake and there won't be anybody there? I can go there whenever I want to, just by leaving my body?"

"It's not that different from daydreaming, is it? But if you stay out of your body for too long, you may not be able to get back." Ginny frowned and picked up a strand of her hair again, tugging at it with thin fingers. "I don't think I should have told you."

"Don't worry about it. I'll be careful. But look, can you take me into your room, too? So I can see it? I really want to see your room."

"No," Ginny said. "It doesn't work that way. I can't take you anywhere you haven't been. If we go somewhere together, it has to be to a place we both remember."

Stupid ghost. I wasn't going to get any proof one way or the other with that dumb rule. "Great. So if flying's so easy, why doesn't everybody do it? Just flit around all day like Peter Pan?"

"I don't know. I guess they prefer being in their bodies." She smiled, shyly. "I remember *Peter Pan*. Mom used to read it to me."

"Read it? She doesn't have to. She's got it memorized. That and 'Goblin Market.' Did you get 'Goblin Market'?"

She shook her head, frowning. "Which one is that? The one about the little boy and the monsters?"

"Huh? No, that's *Where the Wild Things Are*." I'd never liked that story, because all the wild things looked like they breathed too loudly. "No, it's the one about Lizzie who saves her sister Laura from the poison fruit, you know, 'For your sake I have braved the glen/And had to do with goblin merchant men—' "

"It sounds scary," Ginny said. "I don't remember that one. Mom didn't read me scary stories."

"You're kidding! *Peter Pan*'s *not* scary, with Hook and the crocodile and nasty little Tinkerbell trying to get Wendy shot down like a bird?"

Ginny shook her head again. "No. I always knew it would come out all right in the end. Mom told me so the first time she read it to me."

"She never told *me* that. Just let me be terrified through the whole thing." Suddenly I didn't want to talk about books anymore. "Let's go to the lake. Right now. What do we do, fly out the window?"

"No," Ginny said. "Not now. Mom's here. You have to go back."

"What?" I'd almost forgotten that my body was lying there on the bed, but when I looked at it I saw Mom bending over me, shaking my shoulder.

"Go back," Ginny said. "Right now."

"But—"

"Just go! She's going to get really scared if she can't wake you up." She bit her lip and shivered all over, once, like a wet dog. "She'll get hysterical. She'll shake you and shake you and shake you, until you flop back and forth like a rag doll and all the IVs come out of your arms—"

"I don't have IVs in my arms," I said.

"I did."

And then she turned and fled through the wall, and

I was alone. Ginny was right; Mom was shaking me harder. As if through layers of cotton, I heard her saying, "Emma! Emma, wake up!" She looked almost as upset as she had when she'd tried to slap me.

I went back, wondering if she'd slap me for real this time because I hadn't woken up more quickly. "Emma!" Her voice was so loud that it hurt my ears, and I jumped the way you do when the volume on a radio gets turned way up by accident. "Emma, wake up!"

"All right," I said, opening my eyes. "I'm awake." My voice came out funny; kind of slurred, like I'd forgotten how to use my throat. My body still hurt, but the pain was distant and muffled.

Mom was pale and sweaty, ugly wet splotches spreading from the armpits of her blouse. Just like Tom Halloran, I thought with satisfaction. "What's wrong with you?" she asked sharply. "I must have been shaking you for five minutes—"

"I was tired, that's all."

"I thought you came up here to study for your math test. What happened?"

"I got sleepy, all right? I'm awake now."

"Are you sick?" She felt my forehead and frowned. "You don't have a fever. How can you be so tired at seven at night?"

Because I was flying around the ceiling with the ghost of your beloved dead daughter. "I don't know, Mom. Maybe it's because I have my period."

She wrapped a tendril of reddish-gold hair around

one finger. Her hands were shaking. "You're not taking drugs, are you?"

"What?" I sat up; my body felt more real again, but so did the pain, and my voice was still weaker than it should have been. "No, I'm not taking drugs. Not unless you count the Tylenol Mrs. Halloran gave me. Look, Mom, I'm really okay. I'm sorry I upset you."

"Will you be all right to go to school tomorrow?"

"Of course."

"You still sound exhausted. Maybe you should stay home tomorrow and reschedule the test. I'll arrange it with Mr. Miller—"

"It's okay, Mom. I'd rather get it over with."

She tugged at her hair again. "Are you sure you aren't sick?"

"No, I'm not sick!" If I were sick the famous doctor would have to examine me, not that he wouldn't do it anyway. But I had to get her off the topic of my health before she took him up on his previous offer. "I guess I'm a little hungry. Maybe I should have dinner after all."

Mom's face relaxed, and she let go of the strand of hair. "I'll bring up a tray. The pot roast and potatoes, and string beans, and some milk. And ice cream for dessert? Does that sound good?"

"That's great, Mom."

She gave me another of those strange shy smiles from the morning. "Maybe you'd better take an iron pill, too."

"Sure, Mom."

She nodded and bustled out of the room, and bustled back a few minutes later carrying a tray loaded with enough food to feed three of the Halloran children. She sat next to my bed and watched me eat it, and when I'd finished she said, "Do you want to go back to sleep now?"

"Yes." I really wanted to fly, but I couldn't tell her that.

Another shy smile. "I'll read you *Peter Pan,* if you want me to."

Peter Pan. If she only knew. "It's okay, Mom. You don't have to. I think I'll be able to fall asleep on my own."

"All right," she said, and got up and kissed me on the forehead and left the room. It was deep blue dusk outside, the loveliest time of evening, and I felt much better for having eaten. I got up and changed into light summer pajamas suitable for flying, and then I got back into bed and went to find Ginny.

◆ ◇ ◆

OVER THE next two weeks, we learned that there was no way for us to reach the lake in a straight line, because we didn't know the same way to get there. New houses had been built on our block since Ginny died, and Tom Halloran's highway now cut through one corner of town, carrying trucks and buses and vacationers headed for larger lakes to the north. I kept striking off in what I thought was the right direction, only to discover that Ginny was no longer next to me because I'd put myself somewhere she'd never seen and therefore couldn't remember. The first time it happened—as I hovered over the Woolworth's in town—I thought she'd abandoned me, but when I went back home I found her curled with her arms around her knees in one corner of my bedroom ceiling.

"I figured you'd have to come back here," she said. "I was right over Palmer Street and then you weren't there anymore—"

"*I* was over Palmer Street! Over the Woolworth's!"

"There's a Woolworth's there now?" she asked, and then I realized what had happened. She looked at me and said sadly, "That's how it works, Emma. We can only go to places I already know."

"Can't teach a dead dog new tricks," I said, and regretted it the moment I'd spoken, but to my surprise Ginny answered with her sweet, infectious giggle. Mom had told me Ginny was kind to everyone, polite to everyone, honest, brave, moral, and coordinated, but she'd never described Ginny's laugh. It reminded me of the triumphant chortles of the little birds who hunted for food at the edge of the water, and I wondered if Ginny had learned to imitate them from spending so much time at the lake. Did I laugh like that, too?

I'd stopped worrying about whether she was really real or not. Whatever she was, she was vibrant and interesting, and I wasn't about to throw away any distractions. The bleeding had stopped, but the bruises continued, and the breathing had begun to follow me farther out of my body. I joined Ginny now at any time of day, whenever I could, but our dawn expeditions had a special urgency, because at dawn the breathing tracked us like a bloodhound. One morning I saw Ginny looking over her shoulder, frowning, as the noise whistled behind us, the moaning wind before a storm.

♦

"You hear it too, don't you?" I said, and she shivered.

"Come on," she said, flying faster. "We have to find the lake."

We gradually mapped out a route that led through backyards and bits of forest still untouched by the highway, past the elementary school we'd both attended, and along stretches of nearly forgotten back roads, rarely travelled except by children and animals, where the scenery changed only with the seasons. The backyards of the established families in town stayed fairly constant, and the ugly brick school would outlast my grandchildren, if I ever had any, but there were few other human landmarks I could share with Ginny. She had lived in a gentler, slower town than I did, a town untroubled by highways. I wondered if she'd recognize the lake when we finally found it, or if we would forever be unable to reach our destination because owls and foxes no longer glided through the twilight.

But at last we got there. Surrounded by trees, the lake we shared glimmered in an eerie silence, undisturbed by radios or powerboats. Nothing marred the water; there were no inner tubes or water-skiers or bobbing bits of trash. This was the lake of autumn sunsets when the chill kept everyone else away, the lake of summer dawns, the impossible lake of dreams. The first time we reached it, we spent what felt like hours flying loop-de-loops above the water, whirling in dizzying circles and alighting in the tops of trees to rest. When we swooped near the surface, thousands of minnows scattered at the shadows we made on the bottom, and the woods rang with birdsong. I'd never been so happy.

"This is great," I called to Ginny. "This is so great. Is heaven always this much fun?"

"This isn't heaven," she told me, and flew off to sit on a tree branch. I followed her.

"Well, as far as I'm concerned it's heaven. I'd sign on for this right now."

"Not if it was all you could do," she told me.

"Well, it's not *hell*, is it? Where are we, then?"

"No place. Limbo."

"Nuts," I said, and pushed off the branch to do some more aerial cartwheels. But Ginny didn't join me, and when I flew back to the branch she looked thinner somehow, hollower, with deeper shadows under her eyes. For a moment I almost fancied I could see through her.

"Ginny? What—"

It must just have been a cloud over the sun, because in a moment she was solid again. "Show me how to do a triple somersault," I said.

♦ ◇ ♦

IN REAL time, back in the world, reality went rapidly from bad to worse. I was always tired from lack of sleep, always sore from the breathing. School faded into a monotone blur, alleviated only by flashes of terror whenever I encountered one of the Halloran children, and my grades plunged disastrously. My teachers questioned me, yelled at me, asked me if I were ill. My mother simply blamed Jane.

"Of course you can't concentrate," Mom told me after

I'd nearly failed a vocabulary quiz. I'd expected her to scream at me; her sympathy hurt more than her anger would have, because it meant she'd stopped expecting anything from me. "You've just learned that someone you care about can't be trusted to act the way she should. Something like that happened to me once, too . . . it nearly broke my heart."

She trailed off, biting her lip. "When?" I said, my hurt replaced by fascination. "Who?" Ginny had always acted perfectly. Did that mean there was another tragedy in my mother's past? Some man she'd loved before she met my father, maybe?

She shook herself out of her reverie as briskly as she'd shaken out the clean sheets that morning. "It was a very long time ago, Emma, and it doesn't matter now. I only mentioned it because I wanted you to know that I understand how upset you are. It's a terrible shock, but it's also taught you how carefully you have to choose your friends. You'll be all right. I'm just glad this has made you stop spending time with her."

Whatever else the fiasco had done, it provided controversy in a town far too hungry for gossip. As my father had predicted, the scene on the Hallorans' front porch soon mutated into a dozen different versions. In some retellings, Jane lured Tad out in the rowboat and tried to seduce him. In others, he tackled her in the woods, dragged her bound and gagged into the boat, à la Perils of Pauline, and raped her. Sometimes he and Billy—present in only some of these tales—both raped her.

New rumors sprang up overnight, like mushrooms. There were dark hints of beer and pot; there were versions in which Jane tried to drown Tad, ones in which Tad tried to drown Jane, and still others in which Jane and Tad struggled in the water, trying to drown each other, while Billy, stoned and drunk, sat in the boat and watched. The town buzzed with dire whispers of pre-teen sex rings, speculations that Jane was pregnant, reports that Tad had been caught masturbating on the beach, and mutterings that of course Jane was loose, since her mother not only approved of sex education but had helped develop the curriculum. Myrna's offer to hold self-defense classes for all the girls in school—and any of their mothers who cared to attend—did little to quiet the gossips.

"That woman's got too many boys," a matronly shopkeeper told one of the town mailmen while I was buying a candy bar. "By the time she had a girl, she forgot what they're for. Teaching them to fight! She wants one of them Olympic boxers, not a daughter."

"Maybe she wants a mud wrestler," the mailman said, handing her a stack of letters and magazines.

"She's already *got* a mud wrestler," the shopkeeper said darkly, and I put down the Milky Way bar I'd wanted. I wasn't going to give this woman any money. Oblivious to my boycott, she went on, "What else do you think Janie was doing, down by the lake with those boys? Not ballroom dancing, that's for sure!"

In the middle of all this, Jane and Billy steadfastly stuck to their account of what had happened, and the saner adults believed them. The Ewmets sent Tad to stay with his grandparents in California until the ruckus died down, but Mr. Ewmet, finding himself and his family under attack, couldn't remain entirely silent. In his capacity as deacon, he delivered a sermon on the evils of licentious youth. One of the saner adults who'd been there said dryly, "Jane may not have been wearing much in the boat, but that sermon was more thinly veiled than she was."

In response, the road repair crew that had been scheduled to fix a large pothole in front of the church never showed up, and Tom Halloran made no effort to disguise the reason. "There are plenty of other potholes in this town that need fixing," he told a local reporter, who dutifully reprinted the statement in the weekly paper. "If Ewmet repairs the hole in his head, maybe I'll get around to fixing the hole in the road. As it is, I think that pothole's an outward and visible sign of inner unbelievable idiocy, don't you?"

The reporter kept his opinions to himself, but a number of other people who should have stayed out of the fray took sides. My mother, predictably, was one of them. She replaced her usual unit on *Huck Finn* with one on *The Scarlet Letter,* taught largely from filmstrips that watered the text down for seventh graders. After the first few days, none of us bothered trying to read the book.

At the end of the unit we had to give oral reports. My mother gave us the list of topics she'd prepared the last time she taught the book, four years earlier. I picked the safely dull subject of the role of religion in Puritan life. Jane, never one to back away from a fight, chose to talk about "Hester Prynne's Relationship to her Community."

"Hester Prynne must have been mad because the people where she lived didn't have any guts," Jane told us, standing at the front of the class to deliver her report. She'd embroidered a scarlet A+ on her baseball cap; everyone but my mother had laughed when she put it on. It was already a safe bet that she wouldn't be getting an A+ on this report. "Her friends wouldn't talk to her any more. They were prudes and cowards." She glared at me the whole time she was talking.

"Guts!" my mother said at dinner that night, as I sat drowning in shame. "That Halloran girl used the word 'guts' in a report about Nathaniel Hawthorne. Can you imagine?"

"Guts is a perfectly fine word," my father said mildly. He was home for dinner after performing a particularly grueling colectomy; he'd walked into the house whistling and hadn't taken his eyes off me all evening. "It's Anglo-Saxon, love, that's all. Like shit and fuck."

"Stewart!"

My father laughed. "Now, Pam, those are eminently expressive words. The only thing wrong with them is that they're not Latinate. Tennyson had guts as surely as you or I do. Coleridge may not have produced much shit, since opiate addiction causes notorious constipation, but all those fellows fucked whenever they could get it—"

"Stewart! Watch your language in front of your daughter!"

"Oh, my dear, I'm sure she's heard worse from her darling little compatriots. And why should I watch my language, when you do it so vigilantly for me?"

My mother spooned more peas and carrots onto my plate, even though I hadn't touched what was already there. "You're starting to sound like Tom Halloran."

"Yes, he's certainly a vigilante, although he probably couldn't pronounce it." My father whistled a fragment from the William Tell Overture and said, "So tell us, Emma, how is your friend coping with her newfound fame?"

"She's not my friend anymore," I said, my arms aching with bruises under my long-sleeved shirt, and shovelled peas and carrots into my mouth so he wouldn't ask me any more questions. I knew Jane thought I sided with my parents, but I couldn't apologize, because to tell her why I'd acted like such a prude I'd have to tell her about the breathing.

"You're growing up, Emma," my mother said approvingly. "You've finally realized that she's not good enough for you. You'll be much happier in school when you make nicer friends."

I swallowed the peas and carrots, which tasted like gravel. Nicer friends? Like who? Fine, Mom. I'll spend all my free time with Ginny. *That* should make you happy.

The phone rang, and my father grimaced. "That had better not be the hospital. I can't digest pork in an ICU. Pamela, love—"

She'd already gone into the kitchen to get it. "Hello? Yes, of course this is Pamela." Her voice was suddenly cold and scornful, the way it had been when she was talking about Jane's report.

My father raised an eyebrow. "Pam?"

"It's for me," Mom said tightly, and carried the phone into the pantry at the far end of the kitchen. "No," I heard her say, vehemently, and then she closed the pantry door.

My father shrugged at me. "There goes your mother,

shutting herself up with the canned corn again. Is math going any better, Emma?"

"No," I said, straining to hear what Mom was saying through the closed door.

"What are you working on?"

There was a hiss from the pantry, something that sounded like, "Myrna, you're not to call here." My father frowned.

"Mixed variables," I said.

"What?" He looked at me blankly and then said, "Oh, well, those aren't too hard."

Sure they aren't, for a famous doctor. "Absolutely not," my mother said. Her voice faded for a few seconds before rising sharply. "I don't want you in this house, do you understand that?"

"Maybe you should go upstairs and mix up some variables," my father said, still frowning. He'd started tapping on the tabletop with his fingers, a nervous, drumming tattoo.

"I told you," said my mother, "you're not welcome here! Don't call again!"

I wanted to cry, and even my father scowled. "Dad, why does she have to talk to Myrna that way? It's rude, isn't it? Mom's the one who's so big on manners."

"What?" He looked at me blankly again, and then his features softened into something like relief. "Well, Emma, your mother has to act as she thinks best. Don't worry about it. They're both adults, and it's not your responsibility. You should be worrying about your grades instead. Do you want me to help you with the math?"

I shook my head and got up to go to my room. On my way up the stairs I heard my mother say, "This is intolerable. Intolerable! Stewart, can't we get an unlisted number?"

He laughed: a short, sharp sound devoid of humor. "I don't think that will do much good, Pam. You seem to keep forgetting that she knows where we live."

◆ ◇ ◆

"DID YOU have to solve equations with mixed variables?" I asked Ginny that evening, as we did slow circles above the lake.

She grimaced. "We'd just gotten to that in math, and then I had to go into the hospital, so I never learned. I always thought they sounded like mixed vegetables. Peas and carrots. I hated peas and carrots."

"We had peas and carrots tonight."

"Ugh. Have you ever been to Disney World?"

"What?" Her logic frequently mystified me. "Of course not. I've never been anywhere except Aunt Diane's house in Ohio."

Ginny did a graceful loop-de-loop, mirrored by her reflection on the water, and said wistfully, "Dad was going to take us to Disney World when I got out of the hospital. He'd promised. I'd always wanted to go."

"He doesn't make promises like that to me," I said. Why did she always have to make me jealous? "But he loved you, so I guess that's the difference."

"I guess so." Ginny shivered. "He loves you too, doesn't he?"

Did he? He'd taught me to swim; he'd made the balloon animals for me, and he helped me win the pumpkin contest every year. But I didn't know what those things meant anymore. He liked me to swim because he wanted me to exercise, so maybe when he made the balloons he'd really been making fun of my stubby legs. Maybe he carved the pumpkins so carefully just because he couldn't stand to watch contests he didn't win.

"I don't know," I said. "I don't—I can't figure it out. Maybe he did once. I don't know. Anyway, he loved you more. He's never talked about taking me to Disney World, that's for sure."

"He must love you," Ginny said insistently. "He must, Emma."

"Why?" She was making me nervous. "It's not a law, is it? Mom doesn't. Anyway, what do you care?"

"He has to love you! Isn't that why you're here?"

"Huh?" For a moment I thought I heard breathing in the distance, but then I realized it was only the wind in the trees. What was she talking about? "No, that's not why I'm here! I showed you why I'm here. The first time I saw you. When I pointed. Don't you remember?"

"Yes," said Ginny, her voice shaking. "Of course I remember. Doesn't that mean he loves you?"

"*What*? That's not love!"

"It isn't?" she said. "It isn't? I thought it was."

She bit her lip and put on a burst of speed, racing away from me, and suddenly I was terrified. What was she talking about? Everything had been perfect when she was still alive. Those parts of Mom hadn't died yet, before Ginny did. I was proof.

Well, maybe that was all she'd meant. After all, Mom had been pregnant with me when Ginny died. She must have known how women got pregnant; she must have been told that people had babies together because they loved each other. Relieved, I caught up to her and said, "It is when grownups do it, at least sometimes. When he and Mom did it I guess that's what it meant."

Ginny slowed down, turning back to face me. "Don't they now?"

"No. That's why I'm here."

Ginny chewed on a strand of her hair. "Does that mean he doesn't love Mom anymore?"

"Of course he does," I said. That was why I couldn't tell, wasn't it? Because he loved Mom and didn't want her to die from finding out? He had to love Mom; that's why I was going through all this. Even if he was mean to her sometimes, even if he'd burned her poem. He'd burned it to protect her. He'd said so.

Yes, of course he loved her, and he was protecting her and I had to protect her too. That was why I couldn't talk about it in the world, why Jane was furious at me, why I was flying around the dream-lake with Ginny.

And it had all started when Ginny died. If I didn't watch out I'd start hating her again, and the time I spent with her was the only thing I looked forward to these days. "Why do we have to talk about this?" I said. "I came here to fly. Come on!"

I dipped and twirled and did a figure eight, watching

my shadow streak on the water below. Ginny didn't follow me, but I didn't care. The wind smelled like pine needles and fresh grass, and after I'd breathed it long enough my parents and Jane and mixed variables faded into insignificance.

◆ ◇ ◆

EVERYTHING CAME back all too vividly the next morning, although at first it started out as a much better day than usual. I was awakened by the ringing of my alarm clock at 6:15, and when the bell went off I thought I must be having a dream about getting up for school. But it was real. There hadn't been any breathing and I hadn't had to leave my body. I may actually have gotten four hours of sleep. Somebody must have gotten really sick at the hospital in the middle of the night, although I was surprised I hadn't heard the phone. I was getting as deaf as Mom.

Marvelling, I got up and took a leisurely shower, cheered at the thought of no new bruises. He was out of the house. I'd gotten sleep, and I'd actually be able to enjoy breakfast. Maybe I'd even be able to concentrate in school.

But when I went downstairs, my mother was sitting at the dining room table twisting a napkin in her hands, and my father was in the kitchen making scrambled eggs. "Your mother didn't sleep very well last night," he told me, "so I'm making breakfast for her. Do you want some eggs?"

"Sure," I said, confused. My mother's glazed stare frightened me, but at the same time I was grateful that her wakefulness had prevented the breathing, and I was intrigued by the novelty of watching my father cook. He broke the eggs with intense concentration and great delicacy, tapping them gently against the side of a glass bowl until a neat crack appeared. "Want me to make toast? Is she sick?"

"Thank you. That would be nice, since I always burn it. No, she's not ill. Just—on edge. She has things on her mind. You'd better not ask her about it."

"She looks weird, Dad. Sitting at the table staring into space like that."

"I know," he said. "Make the toast, Emma."

"I don't think she even saw me when I came downstairs. Are you sure she's okay?"

"Whole wheat, sweetheart. With lots of butter. You know how I like it."

"Mom likes rye," I told him.

"Make some of that too, then."

"Will she be able to go to school?"

"Of course I'll be able to go to school," my mother said from the kitchen doorway. "Stewart, you'd better do a more thorough job of whipping those eggs before you pour them into the pan."

"Oh, heavens! I guess you've recovered just in time to salvage the meal. Emma, we'd better clear out of here and let your mother cook."

"Are you okay?" I asked her. The effects of a sleepless night showed; she wasn't ruddy under the best of circumstances, but now her skin was chalky, except for the circles under her eyes. She was wearing an unironed blouse, and her hair looked as if small, dirty animals had been burrowing in it. "We can make breakfast, Mom."

"It's all right," she said, looking through me. "I'll do it. He always burns the toast."

"I don't. I'm good at making toast."

"Your sister was good at making toast," she said, and started to cry.

She's dying, I thought. She's dying and I didn't even tell anybody, did I? But maybe I did. I shouldn't have told Myrna that my body wouldn't get used to it and that I didn't want to go home. I shouldn't have eaten with the Hallorans so often. I should have kept my grades up even though I've been spending so much time with Ginny. She's figured it out, and now she'll die.

"Is she dying?" I said.

My father sighed. "Oh, Jesus! No, she's not dying. She's just upset. She is *not* dying, Emma. Everything's going to be all right."

"I'm sorry," Mom said, sniffling. "I'm sorry. I shouldn't be the fool of loss, I know I shouldn't. I'll be all right in a minute."

My father grimaced and started massaging her neck. "Pamela, would you please take some expert medical advice and take a Valium?"

"I hate Valium," she said, wiping her eyes.

"I know you do." He moved from her neck to her shoulders. "That's why I haven't given you any since the funeral, which is the last time you acted this way. But you're coming unravelled and it's scaring Emma, and it's not making me very happy either. Please, Pam? You can't teach like this. You know you can't."

She smiled wanly. "Behold me, for I cannot sleep, a weight of nerves without a mind."

My father raised an eyebrow and cleared his throat. "Pam—"

"All right, Stewart. It was just a quotation. Give me your pill."

He brought her a pill from the medicine cabinet, and she swallowed it without a murmur. Mom never took pills; she hardly even took aspirin. Was she going to turn into a drug addict now? That was one way people died.

She looked up from washing the pill down with orange juice, and saw me staring at her. "I'm fine, Emma." She didn't sound fine, and I wasn't reassured. "Go make the toast. You still have to get ready for school."

I was as ready for school as I was going to get, which wasn't saying much, because to stop worrying about Mom I had to space out even more than usual. I glided through social studies in a fog, and was roused only by the teacher yelling at me. "Emma! Emma, wake up!"

I opened my eyes with a start. Where had I been? At the lake. No, not quite. Somewhere over the woods, on my way to the lake, trying to find Ginny . . .

"Emma, what's the matter with you?"

"Huh?" I said. Everyone was staring at me. "Nothing. I didn't sleep well last night, is all. Guess I'm tired."

"Do you want to go to the nurse?" He stood over me, looking helpless, and I felt sorry for him because he didn't understand anything and he didn't have a lake to go to when life got horrible.

"No," I said. I wasn't about to get anywhere near

Myrna, not after the fight she'd had with my mother. "I'm sorry. I'll pay attention now, really. What were you talking about?"

"Rivers," he said despairingly. "You didn't hear a word, did you? We were talking about how rivers were roads for the early American settlers."

"That's pretty interesting," I said. "What were lakes?"

"Parking lots," said Billy, behind me, and everyone laughed. The teacher shook his head and went back to writing on the board. I felt a tap on the small of my back and jumped, but it was only Billy passing me a note. "Yo, space cadet," it read, in his large, messy handwriting. "Jane won't hate you forever just because your mom's a witch. Here's something I bet you don't know: Jane gave Tad shit in the boat for calling you fat, and he said he liked skinny girls and that's when he tried to touch her."

I blinked at the piece of paper. Jane had stuck up for me after all, and that's why she'd gotten into trouble. My mother and all those people were saying mean things about her because of something that wouldn't have happened if it hadn't been for me. I'd taken her to the lake in the first place, and if she hadn't defended me to Tad, maybe he wouldn't have touched her at all. Maybe he just would have looked at her.

But instead the other thing had happened, and then she'd come home and I'd tattled on her to her mother. Billy was wrong: Jane would hate me forever. I'd hate myself forever.

Billy tapped me again and passed me a second note.

"I thought that might cheer you up, but don't tell anybody or they'll put it in the paper. What's going on with you, anyway?"

"Nothing," I wrote on the bottom, as neatly as I could, and passed it back to him. It came back again a few minutes later.

"You really look rotten," it said. "You should go see Jane's mom. She likes you."

I always looked rotten, because I was fat. "Mind your own business," I wrote, and passed him the crumpled piece of paper. It didn't come back again.

♦ ◊ ♦

I TRIED to stay in my body after that, so people wouldn't keep asking me questions, but it was nearly impossible. Health class consisted of a boring lecture about anorexia, hardly anything I had to worry about. I dozed in my seat, paying only enough attention to know when to gaze alertly at the teacher. In art I played dreamily with clay, and when the teacher asked me what I was making I said, "An abstract sculpture." In math the teacher solved equations with mixed variables while Jane threw spitballs at my back; I escaped all of it by thinking about Disney World. Would my father promise to take us there, if Mom was dying?

And then, blessedly, came lunch. I'd taken to spending it curled in a chair in the school library, supposedly reading but actually soaring above the lake. Today, even more than usual, I couldn't wait to get there, but the lake seemed cloudy, as if a storm was coming, and when Ginny joined me she frowned and said, "You look lousy."

"Yeah," I told her, remembering Billy's cruel concern that morning, "everybody's telling me that. So what else is new? I can't help it if I'm not beautiful. You were the beautiful one. Be grateful. Anyway, you don't look so good yourself."

She'd gotten very pale, the way Mom had been that morning, the way ghosts are supposed to be, and the wind from the water was too cold. "When Mom found out she was going to have you, she said she hoped she'd have another beautiful baby. I told her not to want that. Why would I tell her that, Emma?"

"Because you didn't want the competition," I said, and flew away from her. Why was she doing this to me? The lovely dream couldn't be turning into a nightmare, not now, please, please, when I needed it so much. "You were probably afraid I'd get too much attention if I were beautiful. Oh, shit, Ginny, I'm sorry. I don't want to be mean to you. Look, can't you please make the sun come out? Please?"

"If you'll talk to me," she said.

"Huh? Of course I'll talk to you. What else have I been doing?"

"Flying in circles. You've been spending so much time here that you can't be doing much else. What about school?"

"Oh, come on! Now you sound like Mom! Next you'll start telling me how you used to sit in bed in that stupid frilly nightgown, doing your homework even after you were supposed to be asleep because you loved school so much. Studying the Atlas with a flashlight under the covers.

'Ginny loved geography,' Mom always says, but I think she just likes the alliteration."

Ginny laughed, and the sun came out. "I loved maps, that's for sure. Different places . . . I hated that nightgown, though. She thought I looked so pretty in it, but I was always afraid all those ribbons were going to strangle me in the middle of the night."

At the word "pretty" her face went slack again, the way it had when I'd told her she was beautiful. She flew to sit on a tree branch, a big one that hung out over the water, and I joined her, wiggling my toes in midair. I'd long since stopped worrying about the fact that I didn't really have toes here.

"Well," I said, "you *are* pretty. Nobody lied about that."

"Was," she said, her chin set; when she was being stubborn she looked like our father. "I was pretty, when I was alive."

I looked away uneasily. "Oh, come on, Ginny. You're the one who told me you're real, right?"

"I'm real," she said. "That doesn't mean I'm alive. You're alive, remember? Don't you have to go to classes or something?"

"No! This is my lunch period!"

"Then you'd better eat."

"Do I *look* like I need to eat? I'd rather look like you."

"No, you wouldn't. Nobody should want to look like me. You need to eat. Everybody needs to eat."

"Ginny—"

"Go eat your lunch," she said firmly, and brought

back the clouds again. "Anyway, somebody's calling you. Can't you hear it?"

"No," I said, but Ginny was gone and the lake was too cold again, and when I got back into my body the librarian was standing next to my chair and calling my name.

"Emma? Emma, dear?"

"Yes?"

"Why, there you are. I thought we'd lost you for a minute there. Don't you like that book? You haven't turned a page for the past half hour."

"It's fine," I said. "Thank you. I have to go to French class now."

"Not yet, dear. It's another twenty minutes until the bell. There's someone here who wants to talk to you."

It was Myrna. My stomach contracted when I saw her. Mom hadn't let her come to the house, so she'd hunted me down at school. "I heard that you hadn't been eating lunch lately," she said, sitting down in the chair next to me, "so I thought I should find out why."

"Who told you that?" I asked, looking away. The librarian cleared her throat, returned to her desk, and began filing index cards.

"Jane told me. You always used to eat with her, remember? Now you don't even show up in the cafeteria."

"I can't eat lunch with her," I said. "She hates me."

Myrna rubbed her eyes; she didn't look like she'd gotten much sleep lately either. "Emma, nobody hates you. Please tell me what's wrong."

"Nothing's wrong!" I couldn't tell Myrna that Jane

had spent math class throwing spitballs at me, or I'd be tattling again.

"You're not eating lunch. You're not doing your schoolwork. It's seventy-five degrees out and you're dressed for late October—"

"I'm fine! Leave me alone! Mind your own business!"

"I am minding my business. If I think something's wrong with you, I have to try to find out what it is. That's my job. I'm the school nurse."

"I'll make a deal with you," I said. "If you leave me alone I'll eat salami sandwiches every day and start doing my homework, okay? Are you happy now?"

"No, because I don't think you are."

I turned to face her. "I'm not even supposed to talk to you!" I said, yelling now. The librarian looked up sharply, and then studiously returned to her filing. "If my mother knew I was talking to you she'd kill me! Didn't you hear what she told you on the phone last night? Go away!"

"I didn't talk to her on the phone last night," Myrna said, frowning. "Did she say I did?"

I blinked at her. Had Mom said so? My father had, but only after I'd asked him. But I'd heard Mom say "Myrna," hadn't I? Maybe I really was going crazy. "That wasn't you who called?"

"No." She made a face and said, "Maybe it was my doppleganger. The one who's been attending black masses and plotting to overthrow the Girl Scouts." She shook her head. "I'm sorry. I shouldn't have said that. Emma, I don't think your mother's happy either. And I can't make you tell me something you don't want to tell. But if you change your mind, I'm here. Now answer one more question for me, please: whatever it is that's troubling you, does it have anything to do with your father?"

I opened my mouth, but I couldn't say anything. My nipples tightened and my throat constricted, clenched with the same fear that had paralyzed me before Jane went out in the rowboat. Don't talk about it, don't say anything, don't tell anyone. I couldn't have told now even if I'd wanted to. My body wouldn't let me.

Myrna, watching me, sighed and nodded. "That's what I was afraid of. We have an extra bedroom, you know. Tom Jr.'s old room from before he went away to school."

"I'm not allowed to go to your house," I said, finding my voice. "My mother hates you. She thinks you're fat and your daughter's a slut and your husband's stupid and ugly, and she doesn't know why you ever married him."

"Your mother," Myrna said, and then stopped and took a breath. "Never mind your mother. The door locks from the inside, Emma. You can stay there anytime you want to."

"My mother thinks—"

Myrna reached out to squeeze my hand. I could tell she was trying not to get angry. "Emma, everyone knows what your mother thinks. I don't care about that."

"She's my mother!" I said, terror coiling in my stomach. I was sweating lakes in my heavy sweatshirt. Myrna was going to call the police or something: I knew it. And then Mom would die and it would be my fault and I'd be alone with my father. People like that go to jail, Tom had told Mr. Ewmet—but my father would never go to jail, because he'd fixed the judge's prostate. The judge would give him oranges instead, and my father would come home and punish me. "I have to care about what she thinks! I have to do what she says."

"Oh, honey," Myrna said. "I know you do. I know. Don't worry. I'll talk to her, too."

"No! You can't! You don't understand anything." If you tell her she'll die, she'll die, she'll die. "You don't know what you're talking about! The bruises are from gym and my father—he yells at me for being clumsy but that's okay—"

"Emma," Myrna said, very gently, "It's all right. You didn't tell me anything. I just figured it out. That's my job." She squeezed my hand again, and then she got up and left.

I sat there, staring at the book in my lap. *Podkayne of Mars,* which was about where I wanted to be. And then I realized that it didn't matter. Myrna could talk to Mom all she wanted to; Mom would never believe her, any more than she'd known what the blood was. She'd think Myrna was getting back at her for assigning *The Scarlet Letter.* And if Myrna called the police I'd just lie to them. That way Mom wouldn't die and nothing would change, except that I'd get into trouble for talking to Myrna. It wasn't fair. I didn't want Mom to die, but all my ways of keeping her safe meant that I got hurt.

After another minute or two I left the library and went by my mother's classroom. Mom had a planning period when I had lunch, so I figured Myrna would be in there with her, and I was right. The door was closed, but Mom and Myrna were both so used to talking to lots of people that they projected even when they didn't want to.

"I appreciate your concern," Mom said icily, "but it's completely unnecessary. Emma's fine."

"Emma is most decidedly *not* fine. Pam, forget politics for a minute and open your eyes. You're not a stupid woman. I can't believe that you can't see what's happening."

"She's having a difficult time adjusting to adolescence. Most youngsters this age do. I'm not in the least worried about her."

"Then you're the only one who isn't. Have you talked to any of her teachers lately? Her grades have fallen off, she isn't paying attention in class, and half the time she looks like she's sleepwalking. She's afraid of physical contact and she's wearing entirely too much clothing—"

"As opposed to Jane, who isn't wearing enough. Maybe you should stop paying so much attention to my daughter and start paying more to yours."

"I could say the same about you, but this conversation would degenerate into something entirely unprofessional. Pam, I like Emma. She's a good kid. And something pretty damn serious is eating at her, and if you can't see that you've got your head in the sand."

"I don't know what you're talking about, and I'd be extremely grateful if you'd leave my classroom. Now."

"Then I will, because if that's your attitude you'll never listen to what I have to say. But if you decide you want to listen, will you come talk to me? Better yet, will you talk to Emma?"

"Oh," my mother said, her tones as chilly as ever, "I'll talk to Emma."

"I'm not sure I like the sound of that."

"I'm very sure that it's none of your business."

There was a pause, and Myrna's heavy footsteps moved towards the door. Then they stopped for a moment. "When you talk to her," Myrna said, "Tell her you love her, please. If you do, that is. She needs to hear it."

Dream on, I thought, ducking into the girl's room as Myrna left my mother's classroom. The stench of cigarette smoke and urine made me long unbearably for the dream-lake, but the bell rang, and I headed off to French class instead.

I never got there, because the intercom came on with a hiss of static. "Emma Gray, please report to the English office."

English office? Didn't she have a class now? No, she didn't, because it was Friday and her honors kids were in with Mr. McClellan's kids watching a filmstrip about Hawthorne. Great. So she had a free period to heckle me, and if I didn't show up at the English office she'd show up at the door of my French class.

No way. I headed straight for an exit sign, out the door into hot hazy sunshine, and up the road to the lake, the real lake. There probably wouldn't be too many kids there; everybody was being more careful these days because of the Jane and Tad incident. If somebody followed me to the dock and tried to touch me, let him. Maybe I'd be lucky and he'd have a knife and I'd get killed. Maybe it would be a really sharp knife and I'd get killed really quickly, before I even felt anything. That way Mom would have another angel to love and I'd be able to get away from my father. Whoever else found me at the lake, at least my parents probably wouldn't.

When I got there I lay down on the worn wood. The lapping of the water and the warmth of the sun lulled away my worries, and gradually the real lake faded into the dream-lake, the true lake, the infinitely beautiful lake of which I never wearied. So what if Ginny was being a pill? I didn't need her. I could come here by myself.

I flew and flew and flew, without getting tired or hungry or bored. I could fly forever, here where it was safe, and nothing could ever hurt me. And at last I noticed that Ginny had joined me after all, and was sitting on a branch overhanging the water. Had she been sitting there the whole time? I didn't even know.

"Ginny?" I called. She sat watching me; I couldn't read her expression. I waved. "Hey, Ginny, come on!"

She stayed there. Exasperated, I flew back to join her. "What's the matter? Don't you want to have fun? Let's play tag."

"I never should have brought you here," she said, and another cloud passed over the beautiful scenery. "This isn't—"

"Isn't what? This is perfect, when you let the sun stay out! Come on, play tag with me."

"Dad used to play tag with me," she said, "but it wasn't fair because he always won. I don't like that game. If all you want to do is fly, I might as well not have come back at all. Emma, this isn't *Peter Pan*."

Yes it is, and Captain Hook's my father and Tinker-bell's my flighty mother, shooting me down every chance she gets. "Yes it is," I said, "because I don't want to grow up, and you never did. We're the lost girls. Come on—you're the one who *liked* the stupid book. Do you think we can find some animals in the woods? Foxes or something? Show me a fox."

"I can't, unless you've already seen it," she said. She was shaking. "Emma, there's only one way not to grow up."

"But—"

"Go home. Go home now, and never come back here again."

"What?" I had to blink back tears, and suddenly I hated her again. Nothing was supposed to hurt here. How could she do this to me? "You're telling me to go away? After all that work? What was the work for, then?"

"So we'd talk," Ginny said. "So we'd share things, so you'd get to know me. But all you want is the pretty stuff. You're just like Mom."

"I'm *what*? Like *Mom*? You've got to be kidding."

"Yes! You're like Mom! Looking for the pretty stuff and not thinking about what anything means! Emma, this isn't a real world. It's just a place where we can talk."

It's just a place to talk, I'd told Jane. *It's not the secret*. But I was scared again, because I didn't want to know Ginny's secret. "And fly. It's the only place I can fly."

"There were a lot of things I wanted to do," Ginny said. "I never got to do them."

"Yeah, so, you never got to go to Disney World. Lots of people go to Disney World. How many people get to fly? I've always wanted to fly, and now I can. Come on!"

I dropped from the branch and plummeted toward the water, only to pull myself into a stall at the last minute. It was gloriously easy. But behind me Ginny, still stuck on the branch like a cat stranded in a tree, had begun to moan. It was the noise ghosts are supposed to make.

I swung back around, the hair on the back of my neck rising. Improbably swift storm clouds had gathered again, and Ginny was clinging to the tree branch, sobbing and howling.

"Ginny? What's wrong with you—"

"I'm dead! That's what's wrong with me! Dead people fly, Emma! I brought you here so I could talk to you, and all you want to do is pretend you're dead!"

"Yeah?" I remembered my fantasy about the knife. "So what if I do? Try being alive again! It hasn't been too much fun lately."

She shook her head wildly. "You don't know what you're talking about. Now go back. Go back! You've spent too much time here."

"If I go will I be able to come here again?"

"If you don't go you'll never be able to leave. You're trapping both of us here. Go home!"

She'd started growing thinner before my eyes, hollower, like something out of a horror movie. "Stop it," I said. "Ginny, cut it out! Stop trying to scare me and be pretty again."

"I didn't stay pretty in the world and I can't here, either. Those are the rules." In the increasing darkness of the clouds she looked gaunt, terror-stricken. "Go," she said, her voice a wail, and I turned and fled just before she melted to bone.

♦ ◊ ♦

"I KNEW YOU'D be here," someone said, and I opened my eyes hoping it would be Ginny, whole and healthy again. Instead, it was a girl nearly as skinny as Ginny, with red ponytails and freckles like mine. If I tried, I could almost see through her. I'd known her name once. What was her name? I couldn't remember.

"Everybody's been looking for you. They've been paging you at school and nobody could find you and your mom's having a fit. I knew you'd be here."

Jane. That's who it was. Jane was standing over me, scowling, her hands on her hips, sunlight leaking through her skin. I blinked, and she turned solid again. Now she's going to beat me up, I thought, my body weighing me down like stone. She's been waiting for her chance and she came out here to take it.

But she only scowled harder, and said, "Cripes, Emma, look at your face! You look like a lobster."

"What?" When I tried to talk the skin around my mouth and nose felt like it was going to come off. I blinked, chasing a vague memory of lying down with the sun on my face . . . the sun. There wasn't much sun now. The sky was becoming overcast, the same way it had at the dream-lake when Ginny—

I shivered. "What time is it?"

"About three-thirty. It's going to rain. Look, come back to my house if you want to, and you can call your mom and pretend you're at the library or something and go home when she calms down."

"She won't calm down," I said. She'll die. She'll melt like Ginny melted. "Did you tell her I was here?"

"Huh? Of course not! *I* know when to keep my mouth shut, unlike some people I could mention. You owe me one, Emma."

Ashamed and frightened, I bowed my head. I knew I should thank her for sticking up for me in the boat, but I was too embarrassed to talk about it. "I know. Are you going to beat me up?"

"Huh? No! Who told you that?"

"Nobody. But you were mad at me, and you kept throwing spitballs—"

"I was trying to get your attention, idiot! Because you wouldn't talk to me anymore. I figured your mom brainwashed you into hating me."

"She tried," I said. The sunburn made me feel feverish, and I kept seeing images of Ginny collapsing into a death's-head. "I don't know what to do. Whatever I do, she'll be upset. She's always upset."

"Aw—look, Emma. She was really scared, your mom. You don't exactly cut classes and disappear all the time, you know. So when she sees you she'll probably yell, but mostly she'll be relieved. Come on: whatever else you do, you'd better let my mother look at your face. We'll sneak through the woods and go in the back door at my house."

"But I'm not supposed to talk to any of you," I said.

"Emma! What, she's going to be mad that I found you and my mom gave you first aid? She'll probably give us medals, unless she's like ugly old Mr. Ewmet. And I don't think she's that dumb, even if she did hate my poem and make us give those stupid reports. Stop worrying so much. Come on. It's starting to rain."

We were both soaked by the time we got to her house. My legs felt like rubber, and my nose and forehead hurt so much that it was hard to keep from crying. Jane led me into her house—she had grabbed the sleeve of my sweatshirt, and tugged at it as if I were blind—and yelled, "Hey, we're here! Mom?"

The Halloran household was in full riot mode: TV blaring, animals running underfoot, one of Jane's sisters-in-law breastfeeding a baby at the kitchen table while Tom Jr. discussed dirt-bike racing with two of his brothers, someone whose back I didn't recognize rooting through the refrigerator, saying plaintively, "Where's the celery? I just want a piece of celery! Anybody seen any celery?"

"In the vegetable bin, dummy," Jane told him. She parked me by a wall and let go of my arm. "Stand there and drip, okay? I'll get you some dry clothing."

"Nothing of yours will fit me."

"We'll find something. Don't worry. Hey, guys, where's Mom?"

"In her study," the sister-in-law said. "With the door closed. She's taking a sanity break and she's *not* in a good mood. You'd better not bother her, unless it's a medical emergency."

"I need some sunburn lotion," Jane said, and started down the hall to her mother's study.

"Upstairs," Tom Jr. called after her. "In the linen closet next to Mom and Dad's bathroom—hey, Jane! Did you hear me? You don't need to bother Mom for that, do you?"

She didn't answer. Tom Jr. shrugged, looked at me, and whistled. "Well. Maybe she does, after all. That's quite a job you did on yourself, Emma."

"Thanks," I said.

Someone's toddler wandered up, handed me a stuffed dog whose floppy ears were sticky with spit, and wandered away again. "Do you want to sit down?" said the sister-in-law.

"No. I have to leave soon."

"No, you don't." It was Myrna, with Jane following her. "You don't have to leave at all." She dumped a cat off one of the kitchen chairs and said, "Sit down while I put this lotion on your face, Emma."

I'd heard her use that voice on her own kids. It didn't permit disobedience. I sat down, cradling the toy. "I have to go home."

"Why?" Myrna spread the cream on my face with firm, gentle strokes. "I think you should stay here. This is an awful burn, you know. You practically gave yourself a second degree."

Mom will give me the third, I thought, and said, "My mother will be mad at me."

Myrna pressed her lips into a thin line. "Yes, I'm sure she will. But she'll also be glad that you're safe. Why don't you spend the night here? I'll call her and take care of it."

"It won't do any good. She won't talk to you. The only thing that will do any good is for me to go home."

I meant it. As much as I hated Mom sometimes, I didn't want the rest of her to die. And home was where I lived, the place that held whatever I had: my Nancy Drew books, my calendar from Jane and my stuffed horse from Aunt Diane, the afghan Mom had made for me, however sloppily. There wasn't anything of mine in this house: just other people's children, other people's animals, other people's food and conversations and favorite TV shows.

Still clutching the damp dog, I twisted away from Myrna's hands and looked out the kitchen window. The rain had stopped, and somebody was on our porch. I peered at the figure, not daring to hope; when she turned towards the Hallorans', my joy was so intense that for a moment I thought I was flying, even though I was still in my body.

"I'm going home now," I said, handing the stuffed dog to Myrna. "It's okay. Everything's fine."

"What?" She shook her head. "Emma, I really don't think—"

"Don't worry," I said, and ran out the back door. Everything was going to be all right, because Ginny was sitting on our front steps.

♦ ◊ ♦

IT WASN'T Ginny, of course, but a woman who looked the way Ginny probably would have looked if she'd lived to be my mother's age: still tiny, still with the same flowing auburn hair, but with lines of laughter and weariness etched around the eyes and mouth. She was wearing jeans and old sneakers and had a black leather jacket draped over her shoulders, despite the heat, and her eyes were the blue of the lake on cloudless July afternoons. She smiled and stood up, extending her hand,

and said, "You must be Pam and Stewart's daughter. I'm Donna, your mother's sister."

"Hi," I said, remembering Ginny's first visit. *I know lots you don't know.* She was real. She was a real ghost, not my imagination, not just something I'd dreamed up to amuse myself. She was a real dead person who'd come back to talk to me, a dead person who'd done cartwheels and melted into a skeleton. My own bones ran fluid for a moment, and I felt goosebumps goose-stepping up my arms. "I'm Emma."

"I guess your mother didn't tell you I was planning to visit."

I shook my head. "Where are you from?"

"New York."

Of course. Macy's. "How long will you be here?"

"Just for the weekend," Donna said. "I won't be staying at the house, though. I got a room at the Howard Johnson's on the highway. I don't think your mother is going to be happy to see me."

I swallowed. "Are you the person she was yelling at on the phone last night?"

"Bingo," Donna answered drily. "Hello, Pam."

I turned around to find my mother standing behind me, glaring. I hadn't even heard her car pull into the driveway. "Well," she said tightly, "I should have known she'd be with you. Emma, what happened to your face?"

"I got sunburned," I said. "I went to the lake and fell asleep. I'm sorry."

"Why are you wet? Don't tell me you went swimming in all that clothing?"

"I got caught in the rain coming home. I'm sorry."

"I was worried sick about you! Don't do that to me again!"

"I'm sorry, Mom." I bent my head so she wouldn't see how hard I was trying not to cry. How sick had she been? As sick as Ginny?

"I even called your father at the hospital—interrupted him during rounds! So he could come home and help me look for you! I interrupted him at work! Do you understand that?"

"Pam, she's here now," Donna said. "It's all right."

"No, it's not, but Emma and I will discuss this later. Donna, I want you to leave. I told you not to come here—"

"Yes, you did. Repeatedly. But I need to talk to you, and I can't do it on the phone. I won't stay long, I promise. May I please come in?"

"No! You may not come in! I don't want you here! You haven't changed a bit—"

"Nonsense. It's been twelve years, Pam. I've changed more than you'll ever know."

"You're still a pushy phony! Barging in where you aren't wanted, with your teenage clothing and your contact lenses and your fake dyed hair—it was never that exact shade of red before, was it?"

"No," Donna said, raising an eyebrow. "It wasn't. Cheap shot, big sister." She dug her fingers into her hair as if she were going to scratch her scalp, and instead tugged until the entire mane came away in her hand. Underneath, her skull was covered with thin fuzz, like the down on a duckling.

My mother stared. "What did you expect?" Donna said. "I've just had a year of chemotherapy."

"What?"

"Che-mo-ther-a-py. Our new vocabulary word for today. It means—

"I know what it means! Why didn't you tell me?"

"Oh, hell." Donna started pacing on the porch. "I did. I did tell you. I should have expected this. I should have known."

"Expected what? Told me when?" My mother was using her grammar-drill voice.

"Dammit all to hell, Pam! I sent you a ten-page letter last March. Didn't you read it?"

"I never got any letter. Stop cursing in front of my daughter and tell me what you're talking about."

"Shit!" Donna said, and pulled her wig back on. "Excuse me, Emma."

"S'okay," I said. Like Ginny, this woman was interesting, even if she was spooky. "You do that a lot? Pull your hair off to freak people out?"

She grinned at me. "Not often, but it's effective."

"Should have known *what*?" said my mother.

The grin turned into a scowl. "That not even you would have been that cold on the phone if you'd read my letter."

"What letter? I never got any letter! What are you talking about?" Mom's voice had risen an octave, and I wondered if the Hallorans were gathered at their kitchen window watching this scene the way we'd watched Tom's argument with Mr. Ewmet.

"I'm talking about Revisionist History 101, subtitled Life as Fiction, Or, Here We Go Again. Pam, Stewart assured me that you had gotten the letter."

"You talked to him?" Mom said. She sounded like the breaking strings on a violin. "You've been talking to him? When? How? You promised—"

"Jesus, Pam! I didn't *want* to talk to him! I wanted to talk to you. He never gave you the message, did he?"

"He knows how I feel about you."

Donna stopped pacing, crossed her arms, and raised her eyebrows. "Well. In that case, I should think he'd have told you I had cancer just to make you happy."

"Donna! How can you say that?"

"Pam!" Donna said, and shook her head. "My God, but you two are a pair. Look, I really think we'd better discuss this inside."

◆ ◇ ◆

"I'M SURE you're mistaken," Mom said. She stood at the kitchen sink, trying to mix some frozen orange juice so we'd have something cold to drink, but her hands were shaking so badly she couldn't get the top off the can.

"Do you want me to do that?" Donna asked.

"No! I want you to tell me what this is all about!"

"I already told you. When you hadn't answered the letter in a few weeks, I called to see if you'd gotten it. Stewart answered the phone and assured me that you had; you were devastated, he told me, and would be in touch as soon as you'd come to grips with my illness. Those were his exact words. I remember them precisely, because at the time I was puking my guts up and losing clumps of hair every time I turned around, and I remember thinking that it was a hell of a time for *you* to be devastated."

"You must be mistaken," Mom said. "I didn't get the letter, and Stewart wouldn't have—"

"Goddamn it, Pam! It all comes down to the same old thing! Either I'm lying or he is. You can't believe both of us, and that means I don't stand a chance, doesn't it?"

A car door slammed, followed by footsteps on the porch. "Here he is," Mom said, looking infinitely relieved. "I'm sure there's some rational explanation for all this."

"Here I am," my father said when he came in. He was wearing crisp khakis and a short-sleeved polo shirt, and looked as if he'd just bathed. "Oh—you found her. Good. Emma, you shouldn't—oh. Hello, Donna."

"Stewart," Donna said. "Did I or did I not have a telephone conversation with you last March about a certain letter I sent to Pam?"

"I beg your pardon? Emma, sweetheart, where did you get that sunburn?"

"At the lake," I said.

"Don't change the subject," said Donna. "Last March, Stewart. The letter I sent Pam telling her I had cancer? Remember that one?"

"Oh, Donna." My father's voice assumed the grave concern he always used when he was speaking to patients with fatal illnesses. "I'm very sorry."

"I know. That's what you said during the phone conversation too."

"You must be mistaken. We never got any letter and I never spoke to you."

"There," Mom said, "Didn't I tell you?"

"You told me she was at a PTA meeting," Donna said, as if explaining basic plumbing to an extremely small child. "You said she'd call me when she came to grips—"

"I don't belong to the PTA," Mom said triumphantly. "You must have imagined the entire thing."

My father frowned. "Maybe you dreamed it. Chemotherapy can give people very vivid dreams."

"Balls, Stewart! It showed up plainly enough on my phone bill the next month. We talked for half an hour. You made me describe the entire treatment regimen, right down to the gauge of the needles they were putting in my arms and the color and consistency of my bowel movements. If we *didn't* have that conversation, how did you know I was having chemo then?"

"Most cancer patients have chemo," my father said calmly. "It gives many of them vivid dreams. Donna, I'm sorry you've been ill. I'm sorry we didn't know until now. What can we do to help you?"

"You can start by telling the truth."

"But I am telling the truth. Do you think I censor my wife's letters? She obviously got the one you sent a few weeks ago telling us you planned to come here—"

"Yes, well, maybe she got to the mail first that day."

"Donna!" said Mom.

"Pam," said Donna. "Listen to me, please. I didn't

come fifteen hundred miles in a wig to watch your husband amputating reality. Stewart is lying. The same way he lied—"

"Donna, I won't have you saying these things in front of my daughter!"

"Somehow I doubt you say much in front of your daughter. Emma, tell me something: did you know I existed until this afternoon?"

"Yes," I said. Mom and my father glanced at each other over Donna's head; they looked as surprised as Donna did.

"Really? What did your parents tell you about me?"

"Nothing. Mom, was that Aunt Donna's letter you were reading when I came home from Jane's house a few weeks ago?"

"What? When, sweetheart?"

"When I fell and skinned my knee. The night Mr. Halloran had the fight with Tad's father. I came home from Jane's house and you were reading something at the dining room table." *You've been brooding about this since last night*, my father had said, and then he'd burned the letter. Come on, Mom. Think. If he burned one letter he could destroy another.

"Yes," Mom said, but she was a shade paler than she'd been before. "Exactly. You see, we got that letter, Donna."

My father gave me an unreadable glance and said, "Maybe you should tell us what the first one said." He sat down at the kitchen table, trying to look casual, but as he passed me I caught an acrid tang of sweat. I'd never smelled sweat on him before, not even during the heaviest of the breathing. He was scared of Donna. I hadn't thought he was scared of anybody.

"What kind of cancer is it?" Mom said, and stopped, and took a breath. "How long—"

"Cervical," Donna said impatiently, waving a hand as if to dismiss a cloud of gnats. "Bad odds, the doctors said, but I've beaten them so far, and I have every intention of living out my biblical threescore and ten. But the treatment isn't fun. It makes you do a lot of thinking, when you aren't sick as a dog. It made me realize that as soon as I was well enough I needed to see you again, Pam, whether you wanted to talk to me or not."

Mom's face tightened. "There are some things we can't talk about. You know that. I can never forget what happened, but I'm willing to forgive you if you'll apologize, just once, for what you did—"

"Pam, I'm sorrier than I can tell you about the whole bloody mess, but I didn't *do* anything. And if the only way you can make peace with yourself is to believe that I'm a monster, I might as well turn around and go home."

Mom made a fluttering, helpless gesture with her hands. "Under the circumstances," said my father, "it would be better if you didn't stay here."

"I have a hotel room," Donna said with a sigh. "I also have a request. You didn't let me attend the funeral. I'd like to visit Ginny's grave now, if I may."

Mom had started shaking in earnest, hugging herself. My father got up and stood next to her, putting an arm around her shoulders. "Donna, we can't stop you. You can go to the cemetery and they'll tell you where she is—"

"No," Mom said. "I don't want her going there by herself."

"Oh, Pam! What do you think I'm going to do? Dig up her body and take it back to New York with me?"

"I don't want you going there alone! We'll go with you! We'll all go! I need to do some gardening there anyway. I was going to go tomorrow. We can go now."

"It might rain again," I said, trying to think clearly through my confusion. Ginny had appeared the first time I bled, right after Mom got the letter from Donna—probably the very next morning. *You've been brooding about this since last night*, my father had said, and Ginny had come back to tell me something about Donna. Was Donna my mother's other tragedy? Why hadn't they let her go to the funeral?"

"We'll bring umbrellas," my father said tightly. I couldn't remember the last time I'd seen him so tense. "Pam, are you sure this is wise?"

"Please, Stewart. Let's just go and get it over with. We can drive Donna back to the hotel afterwards."

"All right," said my father. "Donna, I really wish—"

"I'm sure you do," Donna said. She suddenly looked exhausted. "I'm sure we all wish a lot of things."

"Shall we go?" said my mother. "Emma, you'd better change into dry clothing first. Hurry up."

♦ ◇ ♦

I SHARED THE back seat with Donna while my parents talked in the front. "I'm sorry I called you at the hospital," my mother said. "I thought—"

"Don't worry about it, Pam. You needed me at home,

and things were slow at the hospital anyway. My most interesting case was an elderly man who thought hernias were large dogs that lived in Africa."

No one laughed. From my seat behind my father, I could see Mom's white-knuckled hands clenched in her lap, quivering. They looked very much like Ginny's hands.

"So," I said to Donna, "what's New York like? There must be a lot of interesting stuff there."

Donna shook her head and touched my wrist once, lightly. When she spoke, her voice was too carefully matter-of-fact, completely devoid of the sarcasm she'd used back at the house. "It's my home and I love it, Emma, but it's not for everyone. It's very different from Wisconsin."

"She means it's crowded and dirty," my mother said tightly. "And dangerous."

Donna made a face. "Well, sometimes it is, yes."

"Full of runaway children," Mom said.

My father cleared his throat. "Pam—"

"Full of little whores. Full of big ones, too."

"I think," said my father, "that we should change the subject."

Next to me, Donna took a deep breath. Her eyes were closed, and I realized that she was doing relaxation exercises like the ones Myrna had taught me for cramps. After a few seconds she opened her eyes again and said calmly, "Thank you for coming to the cemetery with me, Pam. I know this is hard for you."

"It was time for me to go there anyway. I go at least once a month. I have to. The groundkeepers just don't keep up with anything. The plot would be overgrown with crabgrass if I didn't stay on top of it."

"She does a wonderful job," my father said. "I've never claimed to be a gardener, and Pamela's brilliant at it. 'Flowers bloom when she walks by.' There's some poem like that, isn't there? All that pruning and weeding and fertilizing in the spring and summer, not to mention watering when we haven't gotten enough rain, and then in the fall all those leaves to rake away, and in the winter she plants bulbs and puts down grass seed. It's really quite a job, that little garden. Amazing how many hours it takes just keeping a tiny patch of soil so fertile. I'd never have the patience for it."

"Ginny loved flowers," my mother said. Her voice sounded raw, as if she were about to start crying. "She disappeared in the dead of winter, just the worst time of year for a journey, and such a long journey. The least I can do is make sure she has flowers now."

My heart sank. It was always a bad sign when Mom started speaking in quotations, and these weren't even pretty ones. My father sighed. "Okay. I give up, Pam. I can't place it. I'd guess Browning if I had to, but I'm sure I'm wrong."

"Wrong century," Donna said. "Eliot, by way of Auden. Tell me about the flowers, Pam."

My mother let out a strangled laugh. "There's rosemary, that's for remembrance. I would give you some violets, but they withered all—"

"Daffodils," my father said quietly. "You planted daffodils, Pamela, remember? Like Wordsworth's daffodils. And there are—what are those blue things that are blooming now? You know I always forget the names."

"Irises," my mother said, in something more like her normal voice. "They're irises. I'm sorry. Look—here we are already."

We drove through the iron cemetery gates and along the winding road I'd come to hate during so many earlier visits. Ginny's plot stood in the shade of an old maple tree, promising at least some relief from the stifling heat. As I moved into the darkness cast by the leaves, I realized for the first time that whatever was in Ginny's coffin after twelve years bore a much closer resemblance to the skeletal apparition I'd seen today than to the charming child whose photographs hung all over the house.

"It's a lovely stone," Donna said. "You chose well."

My mother nodded. "We wanted something simple."

I'd always wondered why Mom hadn't insisted on a mausoleum, or at least a wrought-iron bench fit for swooning. The restraint embodied in Ginny's tombstone seemed unlike her. But for whatever reason, there it was: a simple gray granite slab bearing the inscription, "Beloved Daughter Virginia Ann Gray: 1952–1964. May she rest in abiding peace."

Abiding peace. My visits with Ginny, once such a source of solace, had become less and less peaceful. The lake was peaceful—that perfect, invented place—but I wasn't supposed to go there anymore. *You're trapping both of us here.* What difference did it make, though? Wasn't the world a trap, too?

Mom had gotten down on her knees to prune some bushes that didn't really need it. She looked clumsy, encumbered. Donna moved a short distance away and stood, hands clasped in front of her and head bowed, as if she were praying. My father and I simply stood there, watching them. It was very hot. Bees droned through the heavy, humid air, harmonizing with a distant lawnmower.

Mom fiddled with some more flowers, her head bent. When the two of us were here by ourselves she abandoned the pretense of gardening and sat there for an hour or more, lost in contemplation; but when my father came too she wasn't comfortable unless she appeared to be doing something, and having Donna along only made it worse. Mom kept rearranging flower pots and pulling off dead leaves long after Donna had raised her head and unclasped her hands.

"It looks great," my father said after a few more minutes. "Really, Pam. I think you've done everything you need to."

"It's lovely," Donna said again. "Thank you for bringing me." She wiped sweat from her forehead with the back of her hand; rivulets were already trickling down my back, and dark circles were spreading from the armpits of my father's polo shirt.

"I think she'd have liked it here," Mom said, clutching her gardening tools. "I think she'd have thought it was pretty."

"Anyone would think it was pretty," said Donna. "The flowers are beautiful.

"And from her ashes may be made the violet of her native land," my mother said softly. She looked up at Donna. "It's a lot nicer than New York, you know."

"Yes, it is. There's no doubt about that."

Mom lowered her head again. "She never would

have been happy somewhere without flowers. She loved flowers."

Her voice was ragged again, and my father shifted from one foot to the other. "Pamela, the flowers are fine. You've done everything you need to do. Donna has to get back to her hotel and the rest of us have to get into some air-conditioning—"

"I would like," said my mother, "to stay for just a few more minutes. If you don't mind."

Her back had gone rigid. Don't argue with her, I thought, don't anybody argue with her or we'll all be in trouble.

"It's fine with me," Donna said firmly. "I'm the person who wanted to come here in the first place."

My father groaned. "Look, dear ladies, we'll honor Ginny's memory just as much if we *don't* give ourselves heatstroke—"

"Ginny's memory!" my mother said, standing and turning faster than I would have thought possible in the heat. "Ginny's memory! What in the world do *you* know about Ginny's memory?"

I stared at her, amazed. I'd never heard her get this angry at my father, not even when he burned the letter. "Good question," Donna murmured, but my father just shook his head.

"Pamela—"

"All of you!" she said. "You're all trying to take her away from me! Stewart doesn't want to talk about her and Emma doesn't want to hear about her and you, Donna, you have the gall to insist on coming here when you couldn't even respect her memory the night before the funeral—"

"That's enough," my father said sharply. "Pamela, just calm down—"

"I won't calm down! And you can't take her away from me!"

My fingertips had gone numb, despite the heat. *All you want to hear is the pretty stuff.* What had happened the night before the funeral?

"Pam," Donna said softly. "She's already been taken away. She's gone."

"Not to me, she isn't! She'll never be gone!" She started pacing back and forth in front of the grave, twisting her wedding ring. "Dear heavenly child that cannot die—mine, mine, for ever, ever mine!"

She was dying. She had to be. She'd never been this bad. Donna put her hand on my shoulder, and my father shifted into his most soothing doctor voice. "Pamela, come on now. I hope she's in heaven as much as you do, but wherever she is, she isn't your personal property. Everyone else loved her too—"

"None of you love her as much as I do! How could you, when you can't even feel sympathy for my pain? If you loved her you'd talk about her, Stewart. If Donna loved her she wouldn't have tried to—"

"That," he said, all comfort gone, the word as sharp as a scalpel blade, "is long over and best forgotten, and you won't do anyone any good by mentioning it again."

But Mom, for once, was in no mood to be shut up. "She thought you were God, Stewart. She thought you were going to save her. Remember that passage from the Bible she showed me the night before she went into the hospital? 'Such knowledge is too wonderful for me; it is high, I cannot attain unto it.' One of those psalms about the wisdom of the Lord, and she told me it was about you. Have you forgotten that?"

"Pamela—"

"That's how much that child looked up to you, and ever since she died you won't even mention her name unless you're forced to!"

"Pamela, what do you want me to say? Yes, I'm a doctor. Doctors' children die too. I couldn't cure her when she was sick and I can't bring her back now. I wish I could! If talking about her could bring her back, I'd talk until I was blue in the face. What do you want from me?"

"Tell me you remember her," Mom said. "Show me we share a common grief. Tell me something you cherish about her, something that reminds you of her, something you miss—"

"Come here," he said, and held out his arms. "Come here. I'll tell you what I remember about Ginny, but I'm not going to have you yelling at me this way."

Mom went to him, stiffly, and he started rocking her. I couldn't watch it; he was making calm *shssshing* noises, probably the same ones he used on bewildered patients coming out of anesthesia—or frightened ones going under—but from where I stood I could see that his eyes were looking over Mom's shoulder at something else, something past me and Donna.

"We'd better leave them alone," Donna said quietly. "Let's take a walk, Emma, shall we?"

"Sure thing," I said, and turned to follow her. Perhaps twenty-five feet away from us, a family stood clustered around another grave. The daughter, fifteen or sixteen maybe, wore cut-offs and a white sleeveless top. She had long legs and big breasts; you could see the lines of her bra through her shirt. She stared at the tombstone while her mother and brother patted her shoulder, and I wondered if any of them realized that my father had been staring at her.

"Poor Ginny," Donna said softly, and I thought she was going to launch into some story of her own, but instead she said, "Emma, it must be horrible for you, having to listen to all that. Is it always that bad?"

No wonder Mom and Donna didn't get along. "Sometimes," I said, my mouth dry. "Sometimes better, sometimes worse. You know. It's just there." Like women not wearing enough clothing, I thought. Everywhere you look. We could all wear fourteenth-century suits of armor and it wouldn't do any good.

"Do you hate her?"

"Who?" Mom? Ginny? The girl in the shorts? I didn't much like anybody right now, including Donna or myself.

Donna smiled at me. "Your irreproachable older sister, of course. *I'd* hate her, if I were in your position."

"No," I said. "I used to. I don't now. I'm sorry she died." Trying to sound casual, I added, "Did you know her pretty well?"

"Well, pretty well . . . or I thought so at the time. Now I wonder. But we spent a fair amount of time together, yes. Your mother and I were friends before Ginny died."

Had they been? But Mom had talked about runaways

in the car, and when she'd seen me with Donna on the porch she'd said, "I should have known you'd be with her."

I bent my head. "Did she ever visit you in New York?"

Donna frowned at me. "Why—yes. She and your parents used to visit once a year or so."

My mother hated New York. *Aunt Donna and I have the same pajamas. We bought them at Macy's.*

"Yeah? So what happened? Why wouldn't they let you go to her funeral?"

Donna sighed and wiped her forehead. "That's ancient history, Emma, and I'm sure your parents wouldn't want me talking about it. I don't think there's any point in going into it."

My mother hated little girls in pajamas as much as she hated New York, and she'd just had hysterics about people trying to take Ginny away from her. And Ginny had loved maps because they reminded her of different places. *There were a lot of things I wanted to see.*

"She ran away," I said. "She ran away to New York, didn't she? She ran away to your house. That's why Mom hates you."

"Oh, Jesus," Donna said, her voice breaking. She wiped fiercely at her face and said, "It didn't take much for you to figure that out, did it?"

I know lots you don't know. "Why'd she run away?"

"She wanted to join the circus," Donna said.

"The *circus*? In New *York*?"

"The circus. At Madison Square Garden."

I stared at her in disbelief. "Oh, come on. Nobody

runs away to join the circus." *You think it's my fault, because I encouraged her when we went to the circus.*

"Ginny did. We'd gone to see Ringling Brothers the year before, and she'd fallen in love with the acrobats. All the gymnastics, and the lights . . . she wanted to be a star."

"She was a star here," I said. "Why'd she run away?"

"I already told you," Donna said wearily.

I don't believe you. "Tell me more."

Donna sighed. "Your parents called me one Thursday night in October, hysterical, because Ginny was missing. We were all terrified she'd been kidnapped or something; it was a horrible couple of days. I jumped whenever the phone rang, because I was so afraid it was going to be your parents saying that someone had killed her . . . but my phone rang on Saturday afternoon and it was Ginny, waiting to be picked up at Penn Station. She'd taken all the money she'd saved from babysitting and bought a train ticket to New York, so she could come and live with me. When I picked her up she was starving, poor thing—she hadn't had any money for food that whole trip, and later we found out she'd been saving her school lunch money, too. It hurt me to look at her. She was so skinny, and she was covered with bruises from bouncing off the parallel bars during practice. She told me she'd been practicing extra hard so the circus would take her. She was afraid she wouldn't be good enough."

Ginny was light as a bird. I swallowed, and my own bruises began throbbing. Someone had killed her. She'd wanted to see the Thanksgiving parade; she'd wanted to stay in New York. And instead Donna had bought her pajamas at Macy's. *I think that's why I'm here.* "You sent her back home, didn't you?"

"Yes, of course I did. She belonged with her parents. But she got sick right after that, got the flu and got pneumonia, and—well, you know the rest. And your mother blames me, because she needs somebody to blame, I guess."

So do I, I thought. "Didn't you wonder why she ran away? Why she really ran away?"

"No. I didn't wonder about that. I thought I knew the answer. I knew Ginny, remember?" Donna was angry at me, but I didn't care. I was angry at her too. Let her take it. If she died at least everybody would blame cancer, instead of me. "Maybe I was wrong. If you were going to run away, Emma, why would you do it?"

Still angry, I opened my mouth; I might even have told her the truth, if I'd been able to, but I couldn't tell her anything. My father's threats throttled me as surely as if he'd been standing there with his hands around my neck.

"Emma!" my mother said sharply. "There you are. What are you two talking about?"

I turned around. My parents were standing behind us, my father's arm around my mother, both of them backlit by the sun. I squinted at them, my eyes watering, and said, "Nothing I hadn't figured out already. Did he tell you what he cherished about Ginny?"

Mom looked at the ground. "Yes, he did. I'm sorry I made such a scene. I do her wrong to talk so wildly . . . let's go. It's been a bad day for all of us."

No kidding. I hated it here, hated it, hated it, and I didn't want to be in my body but I couldn't bear the thought of facing Ginny again, gaunt, skeletal Ginny who had died. *Ginny was light as a bird.*

"Yes, it has," my father said. "We'll drop Donna at her hotel and have a quiet dinner at home."

"No," Mom said. "Wait—" She stopped, drew a breath, and said, "Donna, do you want to have dinner with us?"

"What?" said my father. He and Donna were both looking at Mom like she was crazy.

"She's sick," Mom said to my father, and to Donna. "You're sick. You came all this way. I—"

"I'd love to, Pam." Donna's voice was gentler than it had been all day. "Thank you. Thank you very much."

"Wonderful," said my father. "Just wonderful. We can talk about the weather. Emma can tell us about mixed variables. I don't know how you two think you can keep from screaming at each other—"

"We'll manage somehow," Donna said, and took Mom's arm. "Come on, Pam. The car's this way, isn't it?"

"I've got the keys!" my father called after them, and snorted when they kept walking. "Christ. This is going to be fun. Emma, don't pay too much attention to your aunt. She doesn't have the firmest grip on reality."

"She has cancer," I said.

"Yes, she does. Crazy people get cancer too. I think your mother's being entirely too generous to someone who hurt her very badly."

"She has cancer," I said. "She could be dying, and she looks like Ginny. She's Mom's sister." Spending time with a dying sister suddenly seemed like the most important thing in the world to me. "Give Mom a break, why don't you?"

"Emma," he said, in a voice like frozen nitrogen,

"don't tell me how to treat your mother. Do you understand?"

"Yes. What did you do with Aunt Donna's letter?"

"What letter?"

"The letter about her being sick. Did you burn that one too?"

He whirled to face me, and his hand was in my hair and I couldn't have cried out if I'd wanted to, and Mom and Aunt Donna were too far ahead of us to realize what had happened. "You don't know what you're talking about," he said, pulling my hair so hard I felt like my scalp was going to come off. "You're a fresh-mouthed little girl and you're in the middle of a very grown-up situation you don't understand at all, something that's a lot older and bigger than you are, and I don't want you acting smart with me or anybody else. Do you understand that, Emma?"

I nodded, because I couldn't talk, and he gave my hair another sharp tug and let go. Nothing that would leave marks, not this time: just burning tears in my eyes, and that awful gag in my throat. *Such knowledge is too high; I cannot attain unto it.* Had Ginny really been saying that he was going to save her?

I don't remember getting into the car. I remember sitting in the back seat while my father drove too fast and Donna and Mom talked about a pet dachshund they'd had when they were little. Mom? A pet dog?

"What happened to it?" I asked, as if knowing what had happened could change anything.

"It died," Donna said. Yes, of course it had. Dogs always died. Everything died. I closed my eyes to shut out the sight of trees and telephone poles going past too quickly, and Ginny was there instead, sitting in her yellow pajamas, curled up in a pool of darkness with her arms around her knees.

How could she be here? She'd never seen this car; we'd only gotten it two years ago. But she wasn't really in the car. She was in my head, in my skull, behind my eyes. What did that mean? That she'd already seen all my thoughts? That once she'd felt so much like I did now that we might as well have had the same memories?

"Now do you understand?" she asked me.

I swallowed. "Such knowledge is too high. I cannot attain unto it."

Ginny buried her head on her knees and shivered like a wet dog, the same way she had when we were in my bedroom and Mom was trying to shake me awake. Had Mom and Donna's dachshund shivered like that when it was dying? Then she looked up at me and said, "Do you know the rest of it?"

"The rest of what?"

"The poem." Ginny swallowed and recited in a thin voice, "O Lord, thou has searched me, and known me. Thou knowest my downsitting and mine uprising; thou understandest my thought afar off. Thou compassest my path and my lying down, and art acquainted with all my ways. For there is not a word in my tongue, but lo, O Lord, thou knowest it altogether."

"He told you not to tell," I said. "He told you not to tell anyone, didn't he? And you couldn't. The only way you could tell was to use someone else's words, to make it pretty, to recite poetry."

"Thou hast beset me behind and before, and laid thine hand upon me."

"You had all those bruises," I said, "and everybody thought it was just from gymnastics. They thought you were practicing for the circus."

"Such knowledge is too wonderful for me; it is high, I cannot attain unto it. Whither shall I go from thy Spirit? or whither shall I flee from thy presence?"

"You ran away to New York," I told her. "And Aunt Donna sent you back home. And then you died."

"If I ascend up into heaven, thou art there: if I make my bed in hell, behold, thou art there. If I take the wings of the morning, and dwell in the uttermost parts of the sea; even there shall thy hand lead me, and thy right hand shall hold me."

The wings of the morning. "Ginny was light as a bird," Mom always said; and even I, the neighborhood butterball, had learned to fly. I remembered the way Ginny had looked at the bed the first time I saw her, the way she'd covered her mouth with her hands. She'd seen that, all right, even if I couldn't show her Woolworth's.

"Did you hate dawn too?" I asked her. "Did he—did he—"

"If I say, Surely the darkness shall cover me; even the night shall be light about me. Yea, the darkness hideth not from thee; but the night shineth as the day: the darkness and the light are both alike to thee."

"You told Mom all that?" I said. "That whole poem?"

Far away, someone was saying *Emma, Emma, we're home now.*

"It's Psalm 139," Ginny said, and disappeared. I opened my eyes. We were in the driveway back at the house, and Mom and Donna and my father were all staring at me.

"Emma?" said my father. "What's the matter? Are you sick?"

"Yes," I said. My head still hurt; I felt like I was going to throw up. Their faces were swimming in circles in front of me, and I knew that if I tried to stand up I'd pass out.

♦ ◇ ♦

MY FATHER carried me into the house and deposited me on the living room couch while Mom fluttered around, looking worried. "I'll be okay," I said. "I'm probably just hungry." But when they talked their voices reached me as if through water, and light hurt my eyes.

"I'll start cooking right away," Mom said. I closed my eyes to keep the room from tilting, and opened them again to find a cool hand on my forehead and Donna standing over me, frowning. I kept getting the eerie feeling that Ginny was hiding somewhere just out of sight, and that if I moved my head quickly enough I'd be able to catch a glimpse of her. But I was too weak to move.

"Would you hand me the Bible, please?" I asked Donna.

"The Bible?" said my father. I could hear his voice, but I didn't have the energy to turn to look at him. "Isn't that a little melodramatic? You've caught a rotten virus, Emma, but you don't need last rites."

"That's not what I'm looking for," I said, and felt Ginny's unseen presence come closer as Donna handed me the old, thick book with its tattered leather cover.

"What are you looking for, Emma?"

"Psalms," I said. I didn't want to tell her which one.

"Yes, the psalms are lovely."

Lovely, I thought. You really are Mom's sister, aren't you?

Here it was. Psalm 139, and Ginny had only quoted half of it. The next four verses were about me.

For thou hast possessed my reins: thou hast covered me in my mother's womb.

I will praise thee; for I am fearfully and wonderfully made: marvelous are thy works; and that my soul knoweth right well.

My substance was not hid from thee when I was made in secret, and curiously wrought in the lowest parts of the earth.

Thine eyes did see my substance, yet being unperfect, and in thy book all my members were written, which in continuance were fashioned, when as yet there was none of them.

Thou hast covered me in my mother's womb. Ginny had brought Mom the poem the night before she went into the hospital; by then, Mom was already pregnant with me. The Bible slid off my lap, hitting the carpet with a soft thump, and Donna bent to retrieve it. "Sleep until dinner," she told me. "We'll wake you up when it's time to eat."

I closed my eyes and slipped out of my body. Ginny was curled up in one corner of the ceiling, looking down at me, beautiful again but sad, so sad. I flew up to join her, misery weighting me like lead.

"I read it," I told her. "I read more of it. You brought

Mom that poem just before you died, and told her it was about him."

She nodded, her thin hands trembling.

"Only Mom didn't understand. You'd found the most beautiful way you could to say it; you must have searched for weeks to find just the right poem, so that maybe she'd listen. And it didn't do any good."

"For lo," Ginny said, her voice quavering, "there is not a word in my tongue . . ."

Last rites, my father had said. Had he seen Ginny searching through the psalms too? Had she been lying on the couch the way I was now, too weak to move? "Ginny," I said, "how did you die?"

She just looked at me, as pale as ghosts are supposed to be. "Pneumonia," I said. "But healthy kids don't get pneumonia, not unless something else is wrong with them. And you were so skinny. Why were you so skinny?"

Ginny was always a picky eater. She plucked at a strand of her hair with thin, thin fingers, and I remembered my health teacher's droning lecture about anorexia. "Nobody should want to look like me," Ginny had told me. "You have to eat." And Donna had said she was skinny even before she got sick, because she'd been saving her lunch money for a train ticket.

And the bruises were from gymnastics. Sure. "You stopped eating," I said. "Maybe it was to save money at first, but after Donna sent you back home it was so he'd stop bothering you, so you wouldn't have to be a woman, so you'd die and be able to get away from him. You stopped eating and you got pneumonia and you died. And he's a doctor, and he blamed it on the fucking flu."

She was shivering again, and I wanted to comfort her but I couldn't. She was a ghost, and I was alive. Nothing I could say to her would make any difference. "Ginny," I said, "is that what happened? Please tell me. Is that the way it happened? I need to know."

"He said—he said he couldn't help himself." I could hardly hear her. "He said it was because he loved me, because I was so beautiful, even more beautiful than Mom. He said if she found out it would break her heart, because then she'd know I was more beautiful than she was. I told him there wouldn't be anything for her to find out if it wasn't happening, but he wouldn't stop. I told him he was hurting me, and he wouldn't stop. 'I can't help myself,' he said. 'You're so beautiful, and I love you so much. Any man who sees you will love you. You have to find some way to stop us, because we can't help ourselves.' How could he do that, if he loved me? I tried everything I could, but he wouldn't stop."

"And so you stopped everything," I said. "To get away." I was glad I wasn't in my body then, because if I had been the rage would have killed me: shattered my lungs, burst some vital artery in my brain, destroyed crucial organs past any ability of my father's to repair them. "You got away as far as you could. You died, because that was the only thing you could do to stop him—and even then it didn't stop him, because he's doing the same thing to me, and I'm not even beautiful. Ginny, he was lying: *it wasn't your fault.*"

"But he said—"

"He was lying! The same way he lied to me! He told

you it was because you were beautiful and he told me it was because you were dead, but it happened to both of us!"

I remembered pointing to my bed, that first dawn I'd seen her, and saying, *It's your fault,* and I was so ashamed that I couldn't look at her anymore. I had to make her understand, somehow. I had to. "Ginny, I was lying too. It wasn't your fault. You did everything you could. You tried to be strong and you tried to be perfect, and then you ran away to Aunt Donna's and everybody thought it was just because you wanted to join the circus, and then you started starving yourself so you wouldn't be beautiful anymore. And then you did the hardest thing there was, the thing he'd told you never, ever to do: you told Mom, and you didn't even do it for yourself. You did it for me, and I wasn't even born yet."

I remembered the balloon animals my father had made for me, those fragile creatures with their pitiful little legs, and how unconcerned he'd been when one of them broke. *Don't be upset. I can make another one, see*? Is that what he'd told Mom, when Ginny started getting sick? Had he gotten her pregnant again because he knew Ginny was dying, because he wanted another kid to breathe on?

I couldn't think about that now, because it hurt too much. I had to keep talking. I had to make Ginny understand. "You told Mom for me, to try to protect me. You didn't need to do that. You were going to die anyway. You could have just died, and been rid of all of it. And when you told her she didn't even believe you. She didn't want to know what you were talking about; she wanted to think you were a poetic little girl quoting the Bible. And so you had to come back, and remember all of it, to try to save me. To stop him."

I'd been talking in a rush, fast, fast, like swallowing medicine as quickly as you can so you won't taste it going down. When I stopped I felt like I'd run a race, and she hadn't said a word. "That's it, Ginny, isn't it? That's why you came back. For me."

"Of course," she said sadly, her voice fading even as she spoke. "Hadn't you figured that out by now?" By the time I looked up, she was already gone.

♦ ◊ ♦

BACK IN the world, there was a great commotion coming from the kitchen. I opened my eyes, blinking at the sudden light, and heard my father ranting. "I told you this would happen, Pamela! Now let's stop the charade—"

"Stewart," Donna said, not quite as loudly but with just as much force, "you were the one who made the crack about your daughters getting sick whenever I enter the picture. If you think that's a joke—"

"Stop it!" my mother said. "Just stop it, both of you! I can't listen to this!"

"Well, maybe you should start listening!"

"Donna," said my father, "shut up."

"No! I bloody well will *not* shut up! I shut up for twelve years, and I'm half-convinced that that's what was eating my insides—"

"Cancer was eating your insides, dear lady."

"Ah, Stewart, compassionate as ever. You're terrified of me and you know it, and if you hadn't hypnotized my sister she'd know it too. Here's some poetry for you, Pam: I'm Stewart's Achilles' heel, the chink in his armor, the weak link in his lies. I'm the truth he can't cut out or intimidate or lull into illusion. He can throw away my letters and deny my existence, but he'll never stop me from knowing what really happened the night before the funeral—"

"The night before the funeral," my father said, "is closed! History! And I refuse to discuss it!"

"You don't have to. I'll discuss it instead."

"Donna, there's a lot more wrong with you than cancer! You want to open that up again? Have a pleasant chat about how you made a pass at your sister's husband—"

"I did *not* make a pass at you, you son of a bitch! You came into my bedroom, drunk, and—"

"Stop it!" Mom said. Through the kitchen doorway I could see her, leaning against a counter, both hands pressed to her temples. No wonder she'd been so upset about Jane. *You've just learned that someone you care about can't be trusted to act the way she should.* "You're tearing me apart! Stewart's right. It's over. It doesn't matter what happened. Stop doing this to me, both of you!"

"Stop doing what, Pam? Stop making you face reality? It does matter. It matters very much, because it cost me my sister for twelve years. You can't believe both of us, and I have no way to prove that I'm the one telling the truth, except that I've never lied to you. Stewart came into Ginny's bedroom the night before the funeral and—"

"Time to leave," my father said firmly.

"—and said, 'You're it,' and grabbed me—"

"It's time for you to leave now. Donna, can't you see what you're doing to her?"

Dad used to play tag with me, but it wasn't fair because he always won. I stood up, dizzy, and wobbled towards the kitchen, leaning on furniture, while Donna talked. "Pam, think: think! What made you come into the room in the first place? You heard me yelling, that's what, not that it did a bit of good until you came in—"

"She heard me asking you what you thought you were doing, Donna. You called me into your bedroom—*Ginny's* bedroom, for God's sakes, do you think I'd try to seduce my wife's sister in my dead daughter's room?—because you had stomach cramps, and then you tried to—"

"Stewart, I'd sooner fuck a chainsaw!"

"Stop this," my mother said, begging. "Please just stop it."

"She's right, Donna. That's enough. This is why we didn't want you coming here in the first place, and this is why you're going to leave now. I'll drive you back to the hotel."

"Stewart, I don't even want to be in the same car with you!"

"Well then, you'd better walk. Because I won't have you badgering my wife, and someone has to stay here with Emma."

"I'll call a cab," Donna said icily.

Please, I thought, no, no, let both of them leave, because I can't talk to Mom if he's around. Please. Please. He was lying: he lied to me and he lied to Ginny and he lied to

Mom and Donna, so maybe he was lying when he said Mom would die if she ever heard the truth.

Please let him have been lying. Please. Please let her believe me when I tell her what happened to Ginny. He's lying to Mom too; he's been hurting Mom too, but I can save her instead of killing her. We can both leave. We can both go to the Hallorans'. Myrna will take care of us. But I have to make her believe me first, because if I don't she won't let me out of the house. How can I make her believe me, when she wouldn't even listen to Ginny?

"This isn't New York, Donna. A cab won't get here for twenty minutes, and by then you and Pamela will be at each other's throats—"

"If you drive me to the hotel I may be at yours."

"I'll take that chance. We're leaving now. Right now. Pamela—"

"Yes," my mother said, "that's best. Go now. Please go."

They went, and my mother sat down very heavily at the kitchen table. She looked up dully when I walked into the kitchen.

"Emma, you look terrible. How do you feel?"

"Rotten," I said. "Mom, he thought Donna was Ginny."

"What? Go up to your room, darling. I'll bring you some cold juice."

"He thought Donna was Ginny," I said again, doggedly. "The night before the funeral. She was in Ginny's room, right?"

"The house was full of people," my mother said

defensively. "Diane and her boys and the Idaho cousins. That was the only room left. I never would have put Donna there if we'd had more space."

"She was in Ginny's room," I repeated. "And she and Ginny had the same pajamas." *I think that's why I'm here. To tell you that.* "The yellow ones with Snoopy on them that they got at Macy's."

My mother frowned at me and said sharply, "How did you know about those pajamas? I hated those things. Donna's been telling you stories, hasn't she?"

"No, Mom! She didn't tell me anything. Please listen to me, Mom."

She got up and started carrying coffee cups to the sink. "I'm sorry you heard that ugly argument, Emma, but don't worry about it. You can't be expected to understand these things. Now go back to sleep, dear. You have a fever. Go up to your room and rest so you can get well."

My room was the last place I wanted to go. "Mom, listen to me. Please listen. He was drunk, right? That's why you got so upset when I asked you if you'd ever seen him drunk. And Donna looks like Ginny. I thought she was Ginny too when I saw her."

She turned from the sink to look at me. "Emma, I don't know what Donna told you—"

"Nothing! Donna didn't talk about it!" This wasn't getting me anywhere. That was why she kept the room locked up, so she wouldn't have to think about what had happened. If she couldn't even stand being in the room, how was I going to get through to her? "Mom, that poem Ginny brought you, the Psalm, think about what it meant—"

"I know what it meant! Emma, you didn't even know Ginny. You don't know anything about her."

"Yes, I do," I said, as forcefully as I could. "I do. I'll tell you what I know about her. I know one of her front teeth was chipped and she used to chew the ends of her hair. I know she wanted to go to Disney World. I know she loved the lake and she went there a lot when you thought she was at the library. I know that when she laughed she sounded like the little birds on the beach, and she loved to watch the animals come down to the water to drink. I know she didn't even like that frilly nightgown, because she was afraid the ribbons would strangle her, and I know she told you not to want another beautiful baby. Why would she say that, Mom?"

My mother was staring at me, because I was telling her things she'd never told me, and my father never talked about Ginny at all. "My word," she said. "You and Donna certainly had a thorough little chat at the cemetery, didn't you?"

"No! Donna doesn't know anything! Mom, I know Ginny stopped eating, just stopped, because she didn't want to grow up, and she got skinnier and skinnier and she got sick and then she died. In anybody else it would have been just a cold, but Ginny got pneumonia because she wasn't strong enough to fight it off. Because she hadn't been eating. I know she wanted to disappear so Dad wouldn't see her anymore, so she ran away, but she wasn't running away from you, Mom, really she wasn't. It wasn't that she liked Donna better than she liked you. She was running away from him, so he wouldn't sneak into her bedroom at dawn and—and breathe on her. Mom, that's what she was trying to tell you. That's what the poem from the Bible meant, Mom, Psalm 139, look at it now, you'll see."

Her eyes had narrowed to slits, but at least she was looking at me. I had to keep talking, had to, had to, because if I stopped I wouldn't be able to start again. "Look at it, Mom! Read it again! She brought you the psalm because—because you were going to have a baby. Because she knew the same thing—Mom, the blood on the sheets—"

The gag rose from my stomach and slammed into my throat. I couldn't talk about myself at all; couldn't, couldn't. Ginny had come back to give me a way of telling the story, the same way she'd used the psalm as a way of telling the story, but it wasn't going to do any good, because my mother didn't believe me.

She turned around and ran the water in the sink, hard, and started washing the cups. "Emma, you're very ill and very upset. I'm sorry Donna disturbed you so much, but she's gone now. We'll talk about all of this when you're feeling better."

"Don't blame it on Donna! It has nothing to do with her, except for the pajamas! You know it's true! Mom, you have to know! You feed me so much because Ginny starved to death! You were happy about the—the blood because—because Ginny never got her period, because she worked not to get it. Because she died instead. And you don't want that to happen to me, you don't, you don't, you must love me after all, Mom—"

Her back had stiffened. I swallowed and said desperately, "Mom, please listen to me. Please turn around, Mom."

She turned around and looked at me as if I were one of the Hallorans' dogs, caught shitting in the rosebushes. "That must be some fever, Emma. How in the world did you manage to invent all this?"

"I didn't invent it. I didn't! Ginny told me."

"*Ginny* told you?"

"She talks to me," I said. "The first time was when—was when he—breathing—in my room—but other times too, now, she—"

The coffee cup Mom was holding dropped and shattered on the floor. She laughed, a high-pitched whinny not like her at all, and said, "Oh my God. Dear Lord. Myrna was right: you're crazy."

My eyes stung. That wasn't what Myrna had been saying, was it? Did Myrna think I was crazy? "No I'm not. I'm not!" I shoved the sleeves of my sweatshirt above my elbows. "Look, Mom. See the bruises? I don't even do gymnastics, Mom—"

She winced and turned away from me, and I had to bite my lip to keep from crying. It wasn't going to work; she didn't want to see anything, and I didn't know what else I could tell her. I swallowed, trying to remember something else I knew about Ginny, anything. "Ginny told me—Mom, when she died, she said you shook her and shook her and shook her to try to wake her up, shook the IVs right out of her arms—"

My mother turned chalk white and backed all the

way into the corner of the kitchen. I thought she was going to scream at me, but when she spoke, her voice was nearly as hoarse as mine. "How did you know that? No one knows that. No one else was there. I found her and I couldn't wake her up and I had to go into the hall and get a nurse, because no one had been there with her when she died, no one—"

"Ginny told me," I said. "She was watching you. She saw it."

My mother was shielding herself with her arms as if I'd been throwing stones at her. She started rocking back and forth, but when I took a step towards her she said, "Stop. Don't come near me."

It was what I'd been afraid she'd say, but the look on her face wasn't hatred or scorn or any of the things I'd feared. It was loss, plain unadorned loss, the kind that cuts like a scalpel and leaves you slapping poetry on the wounds. I knew then that she believed me, whether she wanted to or not, and I knew that what hurt more than anything else was that I'd seen Ginny and she hadn't.

"She had to come to me," I said. I tried to say it gently, but it didn't work, because I was too frantic to get out of the house. "Don't you understand? She came to me because you wouldn't listen to her."

She didn't answer me, just stood there rocking herself. She still wouldn't look at me. "Mom, we have to go to Jane's house now. He's lying to you too. He took Ginny away from you. He took Donna away from you. We'll be safe at the Hallorans', Mom. We can stay in one of their extra bedrooms, Myrna already said so, it's got a lock on the door and everything. He won't be able to get us there. Please, Mom. Mom?"

She raised her head and looked at me just as I heard my father's car pull into the driveway. "At the cemetery this afternoon," she said in her fine clear schoolteacher's voice, as if she were explaining a difficult grammatical point, "your father told me that he loved the way Ginny smelled. He said she smelled like soap and baby shampoo and warm milk, and sometimes like peanut butter."

Then she started shaking, hugging herself, shivering the way Ginny had shivered in the pool of darkness. "Mom," I said, terrified, "Mom, you aren't going to die, are you? Please promise me you won't die."

She didn't answer me. She was still shivering when my father walked in and found us there, huddled at opposite ends of the kitchen.

♦ ◇ ♦

"WELL," he said sourly, looking at us, "Donna's certainly gotten everyone thoroughly upset. Pamela, you never should have invited her back to the house."

Mom opened her mouth, closed it, nodded and turned back to the dishes. She was moving in slow motion. My father stared at her. "Pam? Pamela, are you all right?"

She nodded again. "Talk to me," he said. "Pam?"

She shook her head. When he reached out to knead her shoulder, she pulled away from him.

"Pamela!" He took her by both shoulders and turned

her around so that she had to look at him. "Pam, for God's sakes, don't tell me Donna has you believing that crazy story. I *did not* try to seduce your sister. I didn't. Never in a million years would I do that. Do you believe me?"

"Yes," she said. She was looking at me over his shoulder, and she looked terrified.

"Good girl. Tell me you love me."

"Stewart—"

"Just say it. Say 'I love you.' Come on, Pam."

"Stewart, leave me alone!" She pulled away from him and huddled against the counter again, and my father shrugged and turned to me.

"And you, *chère enfant*? Getting your soap opera fix? We don't even need a television here, do we? How are you feeling, anyway?"

"Fine," I said. "I'm going over to Jane's house now."

"No," he said decisively, "I don't think so. I want to take your temperature."

"I'm going to—"

"Emma, you're ill. The Hallorans may not be good neighbors, but I can't in good conscience have you giving them the flu. If you *don't* have a temperature, you can go over there. Okay? Deal? Now wait here."

He left the kitchen. "Mom," I said. "Mom, please—"

"Shhhhh. He's right about the fever. Come here, Emma."

"But—"

"Come here," she said, and I did and she hugged me, put her arms around me and held me. It would have felt wonderful, if it hadn't been so useless. All the times I'd wanted her to hug me, and she was doing it now, when it wouldn't do any good in the world.

"Mom—"

"I'll talk to him."

"*No*! You can't—"

"Hush," she said, just as my father came back into the kitchen carrying an oral thermometer and a small plastic bottle.

"Emma, open your mouth. Pam, sit down and take one of these—"

"Stewart, I don't want to."

"I know you don't, but it's important. You didn't get any sleep last night. Everything will seem much more manageable when you've had some rest."

I stood with the cold glass rod in my mouth, watching helplessly while my father guided her to the table, while Mom docilely swallowed the pill he'd given her. How could she let him give her a sleeping pill? She was just running away, running away from the truth the same way I'd run away. She wasn't going to do anything.

My father took the thermometer out of my mouth. "A hundred and one. That's about what I thought. Okay, kid: two aspirin and into bed."

"I want to go to Jane's."

"Absolutely not. You're sick."

"Mom—"

"Do what he says, Emma. Go up to your room and change into your nightgown, and don't forget to clean out your pockets. I don't want melted bubblegum in the dryer again. Go on, sweetheart."

I didn't have bubblegum in my pockets. How could she sit there and talk about laundry? I wanted to bolt out the back door, but my father was between me and the hall. If I went to my room, could I climb out the window? The lilac tree would never hold me. How many bones would I break if I jumped? Too many for me to crawl to the Hallorans', probably.

Clean out your pockets, I thought bitterly as I climbed the stairs. Great. Maybe she put a parachute in your pocket when she was hugging you, so you can escape from the second floor. Sure. My mom, secret agent. Faster than a speeding couplet. Able to leap tall tombstones in a single bound. Dream on. She wouldn't be able to do anything, once the pill started working. She'd be passed out like the Lady of Shalott.

I put my hand in my pocket and nearly tripped, missing a step. A folded piece of paper. Old notes from math class? A Tennyson poem to comfort me? I pulled it out; it was dirty, and there was something hard wrapped inside it. Money? But it was the wrong shape.

On the second-floor landing, I stopped and unfolded the piece of paper. There was a key inside, and only one room in the house had a working lock.

◆ ◇ ◆

I WAS AFRAID the door wouldn't open after twelve years, but the key turned easily enough. I made sure the lock was bolted securely behind me before I looked at the room.

I don't know what I'd expected—skulls and skeletons maybe, a pot of gold in the middle of the room, a shimmering gateway to the Neverland; but it was just a room, not much larger than mine, covered in a gray, furry blanket of dust. The shades over the windows blocked out a lot of light, but enough came in around the edges for me to make out a small bed, a dresser, bookshelves, a closet door slightly open. Two shelves on the wall held trophies and a collection of dolls, frozen in their foreign clothing.

Struggling not to cough from the dust, I took a step forward. The floor slid and wavered when I moved, but that must have been from the fever. Trapped and helpless, the dolls stared at me from their shelf; their painted eyes pleaded, although I didn't know for what. To be taken down, maybe, dusted off, admired, carried out into the world to be played with and cherished. I wondered if Ginny had played with them, or if they'd been dusty even when she was alive. They looked like the kind of dolls people bring you as gifts: ornate, expensive dolls suited only for display. On the shelf above them, the trophies gleamed dully through their dust. There were ten of them, in different sizes, many crowned with tiny acrobats as frozen as the dolls.

I turned to examine the top of the dresser, and

gingerly reached out to dust off a small silver hand mirror, a comb, a beaded baby bracelet that spelled out "Ginny" in faded letters. It had been the first thing she remembered after I said her name. I tried to put it on, but it was far too small for me.

The bookshelves, then. Books only came in one size. *Peter Pan*, of course, and *The Little Mermaid* and *Little Women* and *A Child's Garden of Verses*, Mom's choices, but next to them were *Black Beauty, Bambi, The Call of the Wild, The Yearling*. Ginny had loved animals. I wondered if she'd known about Mom and Donna's dachshund.

Next to the animal books were books about gymnastics, a book about the Olympics, a thick volume entitled *The History of the Circus*. I pulled it off the shelf. On the title page, Mom had written in her clean, elegant script, "For my dearest Ginny on her eleventh birthday, with love always." I put the book back; the Atlas was next, but I didn't want to touch it. It held too many places where Ginny had never been able to go.

The closet. I nudged the door further open with my foot, wondering if I'd find the yellow Snoopy pajamas, but all I saw were dresses and jumpers and blouses, plaids and flowered prints, clothing that had probably been pretty once but now looked only dingy and out of fashion. There was a skirt with a poodle on it that must have been a museum piece even when Ginny was still alive. All of the clothing looked as if it would disintegrate if I touched it. Well, of course. No one had worn it for—

Twelve years. My knees weakened, and I sat down

on the bed. No one had been in this room for twelve years. If Ginny had lived she'd be twenty-four now, out of school, living somewhere else, and this room would be very different, like the rooms of the Hallorans' grown children. There'd be college pennants on the walls, photographs of proms, graduations, football games. There'd be textbooks and yearbooks; there'd be more trophies. Ginny would have a job and maybe I'd visit her on weekends, or she'd come back on weekends to see us, and she'd bring me presents and take me shopping and teach me things. We'd have slumber parties in this room, just the two of us, and talk all night without being afraid of dawn, without being afraid of hearing—

A key turn in the lock. I froze, as paralyzed as the dolls. Did Mom have another key? But Mom was surely asleep by now, lulled by drugs.

It was my father. When I saw him my stomach shriveled and I cowered back into the dusty coverlet. "You forgot to take your aspirin," he said, holding up a glass of water. I didn't move; he shrugged and put the glass down on the dresser, wiping a space clean for the two white tablets. Then he shut the door, locked it, put the key in his pocket and smiled at me.

"So, what do you think of Ginny's room? It needs a good dusting, wouldn't you say?"

I didn't answer him. I couldn't. He shrugged, beginning to look annoyed, and said, "Really, Emma, I wish you'd stop staring at me like that. I couldn't very well let your mother put a lock on this door without having a key made for myself, could I? What if she'd locked herself in here and gotten sick? What if she passed out in here and no one could get in to help her? That would be terrible, wouldn't it? She might die in here, and no one would be able to get inside."

I swallowed. Was she dying downstairs? If she were dying he'd be trying to help her, wouldn't he? But if I asked him to check, he'd know I'd told her. "Where is she?" I said instead.

"Sleeping downstairs on the couch," he said. "She didn't even make it upstairs to the bedroom. That was a good strong sleeping pill I gave her. She needed to rest. She was very upset. Do you know why?"

"Because of Donna," I said. It came out in a whisper.

"Is that why? I thought it was strange that she was so upset when I got back. I thought she'd be happier once Donna was out of the house." He took a step closer and said, "What were you talking about while I was gone?"

I couldn't back up any farther; I was already pressed against the wall. "Nothing."

"Really? You didn't say anything to upset her? Are you sure?"

"Yes," I said, but the lie stuck in my throat, and I felt my eyes filling with tears. I ached with fever and exhaustion.

"Really? Why did you come in here, Emma?"

"I wanted to see what was in Ginny's room."

"Yes, of course you did. You must have been very curious about it. I understand that. But I don't think you should have stolen your mother's key, do you?"

The tears spilled over. "I didn't steal it, Dad!"

Stupid, stupid. I was reacting exactly the way he

wanted me to, like an animal being driven towards a trap. I'd have stolen the key in a minute if I'd known where she'd had it hidden. But if I admitted to stealing, he'd have a reason to punish me. My nipples began throbbing, and I drew my knees up to my chest and hugged myself.

My father raised an eyebrow. "No? You didn't take it? She *gave* you the key? I find that very difficult to believe. She hates this room. Why would she give you the key, Emma?"

Because I'd told her about Ginny. But I couldn't very well tell him that. And if I said she'd given it to me of her own free will, he might figure out that she'd wanted me to be safe in a locked room, and then he'd know I'd told her. I swallowed, trying to think through my fear, and said, "Because I asked her for it."

"You *asked* her for it? When you know how she feels about this room? No wonder she was so upset when I got home. That wasn't very sensitive of you, Emma, was it?"

Trapped, trapped: the steel jaws sprung. He was making it all my fault. He took another step towards me, his breathing deepening almost imperceptibly, and said, "You played on her emotions, didn't you? She was too upset to refuse you anything because she felt guilty about Donna and Ginny. And so you went and asked her for exactly the one thing that would remind her of both of them, all over again. You were listening to the argument in the kitchen, weren't you? Pretending to be sick. Pretending to be asleep. Little faker. Is that what happened?"

"Yes," I said. I had to get past him. I had to unlock the door. "I'll tell Mom I'm sorry," I said, standing up. "I'll go tell her right now."

"No, you won't. She's asleep. She wouldn't hear you." Another step; the breathing got louder. He was too close to me, and something was growing under his belt. "You're a very sneaky, selfish little girl, Emma. You've upset your mother very badly, and her health suffers when she's upset."

For a moment anger flared through me, consuming my fear in a sudden, welcome hatred. "So did Ginny's," I said. "But that one's your fault, isn't it?"

"*My* fault? Would you like to tell me what you mean by that?"

My throat constricted again, the brief bonfire replaced by ashes and choking fumes. What had I said? How could I have said that? He was bigger than I was. I tried to dart around him, but he grabbed me and threw me back onto the bed, holding me pinned by both arms. I lay there, paralyzed, unable even to struggle. "Answer me, Emma. What did you mean?"

"Nothing, Dad. Nothing, I didn't mean any—"

"*Answer me.*" His hands tightened on my upper arms. "Who's been telling you lies about Ginny?"

I went numb, then. I wanted to leave my body, but I couldn't. It was as if I was stuck half in and half out, unable to get safely away because the part that stayed behind, that remained under my father's hands and answered his questions, had forgotten how to run. It had discovered that it could answer his questions and still tell the truth; and it stayed there, entranced, like a child who persists in mastering the fatal art of lighting matches. "Nobody's been telling me lies about her," it said proudly.

"No? You've been making them up on your own, like your aunt? Your aunt's crazy, you know. That's what happens to women in your mother's family. They get themselves upset over things they've imagined, and then they get sick and they die. Your aunt imagined that I did something to her in Ginny's room, and now she has cancer. Your mother's been on the edge about Ginny for years now, and this latest business with Donna has pushed her over. That's why she couldn't sleep last night, and it's making her sick. See how it works? Don't get yourself too upset over things, Emma."

"Really?" said my body, as the rest of me watched in despair. Liar. Lousy rotten stinking liar. He burned the letter. You know he burned the letter. Ginny was telling the truth. She told you about Donna, and she was right.

"Yes. Really, Emma. That's how it works."

Come on, I told the part of myself that kept talking. Come on. You have to get out of there. I remembered a story about somebody who'd been killed because the end of her scarf got slammed in a car door. She must have felt the way I did now, tugging, tugging, frantically trying to get free of something much larger and more powerful than she was.

I had to find Ginny. I had to go to the lake. But the part of me that had stayed behind said dreamily, wonderingly, "What happened to Ginny, then? What did she imagine you did to her in her room? The same thing you're doing to me now? Is this what you did to Donna?"

"You little bitch," my father said, and slapped me across the mouth. The blow jolted me all the way back into my body, into that achy, wavery place where everything was ugly, where nothing seemed real but the taste of blood in my mouth and the reawakened torment of my sunburn. I looked up at my father's face and saw in amazement that his cheeks were wet, his shoulders shaking. He was sobbing, breathing in deep, shuddering gasps.

"Pneumonia killed her. Pneumonia! We did everything we could. She had the best medical care available. She couldn't have gotten better treatment in Chicago—"

"She could have gotten better treatment in her bedroom," I said. "Let go of me!"

I twisted away from him and started crawling to the door, but he caught me and slapped me again, a stinging blow that reverberated through my skull. His momentary grief had crystallized into rage. "Where do you think you're going, Emma? You can't get away from me. Don't you know that by now?"

Quiet, I told myself. Just stay quiet and take it, and everything will be over with more quickly. But the part that had been talking before wouldn't shut up. "Yes, I can."

"Where?" he said, and shook me. "Where do you think you can go?"

"The same place Ginny went," I said, and fled, dragging the chatterbox dummy with me. Out of this body, right now. It wasn't going to last long, anyhow. Surely he'd kill me. He had to kill me, now, because I knew about Ginny, and he wouldn't be safe unless I was dead too. Anyone doing an autopsy would know what had happened, but doctors stick together. He'd keep them quiet about it. He'd tell them some lie and make them believe it. No one was going to touch him. Not him.

But even when I was out, safe from his hands, the breathing tossed me around the room as if I were only a rubber duck in a gale. "Ginny?" I said, screaming over the storm and fighting to get to the window. If I could get outside I could go to the lake. I'd be safe there. "Ginny, please help me. I need you. Ginny!"

She didn't come. She had to come. "Ginny! Ginny, where are you?"

She wasn't there. She wasn't there. She'd done what she was supposed to do, what she'd come back for: she'd remembered, and she'd told me what she remembered, and she'd gotten me to tell it too. And then she'd gone away again, back to the land where children forget their names.

And I could go there as surely as she had. I knew it, and my father knew it. I could go where Ginny had gone, where I wouldn't have to feel anything anymore, where I'd always be safe from the evil men and the crocodiles, safe with the other lost children.

But it hadn't worked even for Ginny, had it? *If I ascend up into heaven, thou art there: if I make my bed in hell, behold, thou art there.* She hadn't been able to stay in the painless place either, not while it was still happening, not before she'd made someone believe her.

If I died, it would just happen to someone else. There were so many little girls in the world; he'd always be able to find others, even if they weren't his. There were girls in the hospital, girls on the street, girls at the cemetery: little girls who couldn't fight him because he was bigger than they were, little girls growing bigger, bigger, getting bigger where he wanted them to be big.

Bobbing next to the ceiling, caught in the currents of my father's rage as he tried to slap me into consciousness down on the bed, I knew that if I died now nothing would change. It would just keep happening, and all the pain I'd put Ginny through would have been for nothing.

So I bucked the gale and fought my way back into my body, hating it, wanting only to be someplace where this wouldn't hurt. I fought my way back in and then I started fighting my father—screaming, lashing out, going for the eyes and the groin.

He blocked me, cursing, but I rolled away from him and started crawling towards the door, my fever melting all solid surfaces to rubber. Ginny. Remember what happened to Ginny, and it will be easier. "Mom!" I screamed, as loudly as I could, letting my fury fill my lungs. "Mom! He's killing me. Mom, help me!"

"Give up," my father said, grabbing me by the back of my collar. "She can't hear you. The door's locked. There are only two keys. If you fight me you'll just make it harder for yourself—"

"Mom!" I screamed, and managed to pull away from him, landing a solid kick on his ankle in the process. "Mom! Wake up! Call the cops! Mom!"

"Fat chance, fat girl." Panting, he grabbed my collar again and started shaking me so hard I thought my teeth were going to fall out. "I unplugged the phones in case Donna decided to call. In her present condition, your mother can't manage modular jacks."

Somewhere I heard a door slam; I couldn't think what

it meant, because my father was talking to me kindly, reasonably, even as he transferred his grip to my hair. "Now just relax. If you relax you'll be all right. Stop fighting me, Emma. You're making it worse for yourself."

I gritted my teeth and talked around the lump in my throat. "*You're* the one making it—"

He slapped me again. "How can you let yourself be hurt like this, Emma? It would be so much easier to give in."

"You taught me," I told him, the words distorted by pain, my brain blazing with fever and rage. "You taught me to protect everybody except myself—"

The slap was a punch this time. "Who are you protecting, Emma?"

Ginny. No, Ginny's dead. Mom. Donna. The girl at the cemetery. Think about them, because if you think about yourself you'll be too afraid.

Think about Jane. Eyes and crotch. Think about water; he gave you that too, water and all its blessings, the way it flows around you, the way it shines in sunlight. You have to get away from him, so you'll be able to swim again.

I managed to pull out of his grasp, my skull searing, the world going black for a moment, and twisted onto my back, kicking up at his groin with both feet. He danced back just in time and let out a bellow of rage, the loudest sound I'd ever heard him make. Winded and terrified, unable to move, I lay on Ginny's dusty carpet.

"For that," my father said, and I thought I heard banging on the door but I must have been imagining it, because no one was going to help me. I was alone, alone with all the other little girls. I couldn't protect myself or anyone else, and I'd never see water again. "For that—"

For that, I thought, he's going to kill me after all. Just let it happen quickly. Let it be over. But instead there was a shattering, splintering sound and the shriek of wood on wood and a ripping noise accompanied by more clouds of dust, and my father was yanked backwards, emitting a yelp like a wounded dog. Tom Halloran stood behind him, my father's collar in one hand and Jane's baseball bat in the other.

"If you touch that child again," Tom said, his face beet-red, "I'll smash your skull in, you psychotic prick."

◆ ◇ ◆

After that, it's all fragments for a while. I remember noticing that the windowshade had flown upwards, revealing shattered glass and the end of a ladder leaning against the outside of the house. I remember being puzzled because the door was still booming, and hearing Tom say to it, "I've got him, Tommy. Go get your mother."

There were sirens, then, and Myrna came and wrapped me in a blanket. I remember leaning on her, going down the stairs and outside into a hot spring night rendered chaotic with flashing lights and squawking radios and uniformed people who looked bored and worried and disgusted. Shoulders hunched, hands over her eyes, my mother stood in the middle of the front yard, peering out at the scene from between her fingers.

Later, Myrna told me how Mom had run into the Hallorans' kitchen without even knocking and grabbed the phone and started calling everyone on that absurd, oversized list: the cops and the Fire Department and the Ambulance Squad, the Poison Control Center, the Animal Hospital. She said the same thing to all of them. "My daughter's in trouble at 357 Spruce. Please hurry. I'm afraid it's too late."

And then she'd put down the phone and dial the next number, punching the buttons with her shaking hands. She was down to the National Guard when Myrna finally got the phone away from her, and by then Tom had already gone roaring out of the house with his baseball bat, followed by Tom Jr.

It must have been the hardest thing she'd ever done, but I didn't know that yet, when I saw her covering her face. I thought Myrna had made the phone calls, and I wondered why my mother wasn't sleeping on the couch. The sirens must have woken her, even through the drugs. I wondered whether I'd really saved her, whether she'd die after all, what I could say to her. But Myrna spoke for me.

"Pam, look, here's Emma. Emma's here. She's safe now. Pam? Can you hear me?"

My mother uncovered her eyes and closed them instead, bowing her head and clasping her hands in front of her as if she were praying. "Please forgive me," she said, in her clear, lovely voice, and I knew she wasn't talking to us at all.

♦ ◇ ♦

I STAYED NUMB through Mom's nervous breakdown and hospitalization, through my father's trial and conviction, through an endless round of doctors and social workers and therapists. For a while I thought I'd never feel anything again, thought my soul had gone away with Ginny even though my body had stayed on earth, with the birds and the wind and the lake. I lived with the Hallorans and slept in their extra bedroom with the lock on the door and somehow maintained my usual grades through the end of one school year and the beginning of the next, but I couldn't feel anything.

I remember snatches from that summer: looking up at July 4 fireworks—the fanciest our town had ever had, because it was the Bicentennial—and wishing Ginny could see them from heaven; going to Tom Jr.'s house for a barbecue and staying glued to the TV instead, because the Olympic gymnastics finals were on. "She's hurting herself," I kept saying as Nadia Comeneci bounced against the uneven parallel bars. "She's going to have awful bruises. Somebody tell her to stop."

"It's all right," said Tom Jr.'s wife, and turned off the television. "She's all right now, Emma. You just come out into the yard and help me and Janie cook the hamburgers, honey, okay?"

Much later I learned that Jane had spent that summer beating up, or threatening to beat up, more than one kid she heard making snide cracks about me; Tom Sr., in his inimitable fashion, protected me from reporters and their cameras. As the trial approached, the Hallorans disconnected their television entirely, so I wouldn't be subjected to the coverage. They told me it was broken. I never wondered why they hadn't gotten around to fixing it.

Myrna used every possible avenue of the social service network to keep me from having to go on the witness stand, although Donna did so willingly. Another doctor at the hospital came forward and shared his suspicions about Ginny's death, and several of the nurses my father worked with testified to subtle, systematic sexual harrassment. But these are facts I was told afterward, rather than things I remember. My only memory of the event is of Donna sitting at the Hallorans' kitchen table, holding my hand and telling me, "He can't hurt you ever again, Emma. He's not even allowed to live in the same town you do. He has to go away and get help for a very long time."

"Three years," Jane's brother Greg said behind me. "Three years of frigging therapy and community service, and then the bastard gets to practice again!"

"Greg!" Myrna said warningly.

"They should've thrown the creep in jail. So what if they fined him? They should have taken away his license! That judge has oatmeal between his ears—"

"Greg, be quiet!"

"Your father can't hurt you anymore," Donna said, holding my hands very tightly. "He can't live here again. He's not allowed to come near you. Do you understand?"

"Yes." I turned around and said to Greg, "It's because

of the judge's prostate, you know. He gave us all those oranges."

"No," Myrna said. "He was very upset. He was. Emma, he agonized over that sentence. I'm not saying he did what was right, because I think your father should have gone to jail too. But the judge felt awful for you. He thought prison would make your father even meaner than he is now, and he wanted your father to get counselling so he wouldn't hurt anyone else. The judge tried to do the right thing. I don't agree with his decision, but he's a good man."

"He's an idiot," said Greg.

"It doesn't matter what he is," Donna said quietly, "as long as Emma's safe."

Even though I'd fought so hard against my father, I couldn't make myself care about whether I was safe or not. I went about life in a fog which lifted only during my visits to the lake, where I kept searching for glimpses of Ginny. The place which had once seemed so comforting was desolate now, because she wasn't there. Later I learned that one of the Hallorans followed me every time I went there, to make sure nothing happened to me, but at the time I didn't realize it. I always thought I was alone; I'd have thought I was alone if I'd been in Times Square on New Year's Eve, because I was all by myself in a place companionship couldn't touch. I'd told no one but my mother about Ginny's ghost.

Myrna finally made her presence known one chill October afternoon as I sat on the end of the dock, looking out at the water. I was supposed to be at an appointment with another counselor, but I couldn't take the questions anymore, endless questions, questions I didn't know how to answer without telling people about Ginny. And if I talked about Ginny they'd really know I was crazy.

"Emma," someone called behind me, and I turned at the familiar voice and Myrna was on the beach, holding up a sweater. "Aren't you cold?"

I shrugged, and she trudged up the dock towards me. It didn't occur to me to wonder that she was there. "Awfully cold out here," she said, draping the sweater over my shoulders and sitting down next to me. "What are you doing?"

"Thinking."

"What about? Your dad?"

I turned back to the lake, into the wind. "Yeah, I guess. Everything, you know?"

She couldn't possibly know, and being Myrna she probably knew it. Instead of answering, she passed me an apple. "Here," she said. "Thought you might want a snack."

"To keep doctors away?" I asked, and she laughed. The little birds pecking for food on the beach scattered at the noise.

"Yes," she said, grinning hugely. "Yes, to keep doctors away. God bless you, Emma. That's the first joke you've made for—well, just for ages. Keep that up, you hear me?"

I hadn't thought it was funny. I pulled on the sweater, a thick one of Tom's way too large for me, and said, "Will it work on all those counselors, too? I mean, I know I'm probably crazy, but I'm sick of them. All they do is ask stupid questions."

"You aren't crazy," Myrna said, and her vehemence scattered more birds than her laughter had. "You were never crazy, Emma. Your father's crazy and your mother may be crazy, and what happened to you was certainly crazy, but you aren't. Not one bit. Nobody thinks you are. Honey, you're sane and sound and strong as God's little green apples, or you never would have survived all that."

"You don't understand," I said.

"No? Then tell me what I should understand."

"You won't believe me."

"Try me."

I shrugged again, and told her about Ginny: maybe because it was time to tell someone, maybe because Myrna had gone to the trouble of following me to the lake, maybe because I couldn't find Ginny and needed to make her real by talking about her. Maybe I was trying to drive Myrna away, or maybe I was testing her to be sure she'd stay no matter what I told her. Whatever the reason, I told her, all of it, and she listened, and when I was finished she was silent for a long time.

"Well," she said, just when I thought she wasn't going to acknowledge the story at all, "well, that explains a lot, doesn't it."

"You think I'm crazy too, don't you?"

"No, I don't."

"It happened! Really it did. Ginny came and she told me the truth, things I couldn't have known—"

"Ghosts always tell the truth," Myrna said mildly. "That's why people are afraid of them."

We sat there as the sun sank lower and the little birds that sounded so much like Ginny hunted on the beach. "I think," Myrna said slowly after a while, "that most of us never really treasure being alive. We take it for granted. I think Ginny wanted you to understand how precious it is."

I shook my head. She hadn't gotten it at all. "You don't understand. Mom was right—Ginny was a better person than I am. She was! She was prettier and nicer and smarter—"

"I don't know if she was or not, Emma, because I never knew her. I don't think she could have been much smarter than you are, though. You're a damn smart kid. And you're every bit as pretty as anyone needs to be."

I wrapped Tom's sweater more tightly around me. I was shaking, and because I'd fled so far from my pain I thought my trembling was just the cold. "She was nicer! She was! She came back so I'd be able to stop my father, and I couldn't do anything for her at all." Little bits of darkness were flashing in front of my eyes, like an obsidian scalpel slicing open the sky. "All I did was hurt her, just like he did. All I did was make her relive the bad stuff."

"You gave her back her name," Myrna said gently. "You shared the lake with her."

"But I couldn't give her anything new! I couldn't give her anything she really wanted! Disney World or anything!"

"She wanted you to live. She wanted you to feel all the things she can't feel anymore. Do you understand?"

"But she helped me! She did all those things to help me, and I couldn't do anything for her at all!"

"Emma, no one can help her. That's what being dead means. But a lot of people are trying to help you. The best way for you to honor Ginny is to let them." Myrna's voice was sharper then, and I realized dimly, for the first time, how much trouble she'd gone to for me: making all those counselling appointments that I never kept, taking me into her house even though I hardly spoke to anyone there.

I bent my head in shame, and Myrna said softly, "You gave Ginny what she wanted by not giving up. You gave her what she wanted by fighting your father and staying alive. And you can keep giving her what she wants by living a full, rich, feeling life. That's what she was trying to tell you. That's what she wanted most of all."

"How do I do that?" I said helplessly. "I don't know how to do that."

"You're already doing it. You're doing it now, Emma; you're doing it this minute, even if you don't know it yet, even if you still feel dead inside. That's why Ginny hasn't had to come back."

Abiding peace. I closed my eyes, and Myrna touched my shoulder. "Come on," she said. "It's really too cold out here. Time to go home for dinner."

◆ ◇ ◆

A FEW WEEKS after that, I visited my mother in the hospital. It was a nice place, a clean cheerful place; when I got there Mom was sitting next to a window, wearing an old denim skirt and a sweater and brushing her hair while she looked out at the birds. "Hi," she said when she saw me. Her eyes and nose were red, and she sounded like her head was stuffed with cotton. "Are you okay?"

"I guess so. Are you?"

She twisted the brush in her lap, pulling out individual strands of hair. "Yes. I am. Don't worry, Emma. Or feel guilty, that's not right, you shouldn't—"

"You don't sound okay."

She bowed her head. "Well, not yet. But I'm getting there, really I am. The doctors say so, anyhow. I've got this terrible cold now, which is why I'm sitting around in my room. Ordinarily—" she laughed "—I'd be at occupational therapy."

"Yeah? Like what? You have to teach people to write poetry or something?"

She looked up at me and almost smiled. "No, it's things you do with your hands. I'm on a strict diet of concrete nouns, believe me . . . Pottery—there's a real studio with a wheel and a kiln and everything. It's relaxing, the way housework was when—well. I like the way the clay feels, and I'm getting pretty good at it."

"Is that yours?" I asked, nodding towards a white pot sitting on the windowsill.

She nodded eagerly. "Yes! It's not very pretty, it's a little crooked and the glaze is uneven, but it was the first one I ever finished. All the others cracked before I could fire them or exploded in the kiln, but this one—"

"Oh," I said. "I get it. It's a metaphor. I'm your whole crooked pot, is that it?"

She looked stricken, and I felt miserable. Tom had helped me carve a pumpkin for Halloween, and it hadn't been perfect and it hadn't won the contest, but that was okay. I still liked my pumpkin, even if it didn't have a blue ribbon.

◆

Maybe that was how Mom felt about her pot. I shouldn't have been so nasty to her.

"Sorry, Mom. I guess I didn't mean that."

"I think you did," she said stiffly, "but it's all right." I looked up again. She was blushing.

"I'm sorry, Emma. That I ran out of the house when you started screaming. I'd thought the key would be enough to—"

"Yeah, well. He had another one."

"I'm sorry."

"Where did you have it hidden, anyhow? I'd been looking for it for years."

"It was in the cemetery," she said. "Under one of the flower pots. I knew you and your father would never look there, but Donna—Donna always found all my hiding places. Even when we were little. That's why I didn't want her going to the cemetery by herself. And I was afraid she'd go back after we left, so—so I took it, when we were there. That's why I had it. To give you."

I didn't answer. She really did sound crazy. Blushing again, she fiddled with the hairbrush. Then she smiled. "I talked to her last night. Her latest cancer tests were negative. She's going to Bermuda to celebrate."

"I know," I said. Donna and I talked on the phone once a week, and I was supposed to visit her in New York sometime, but I didn't want to tell Mom that yet. "So, do they make you talk to shrinks?"

"Yes. Of course. Doctors and the other patients and myself. That's why I'm here. The rest is just to pass time."

"Yeah," I said. "I'm seeing shrinks too." And talking to myself a lot, but I didn't say that. "Do you like yours?"

"Well, no. But they aren't here to be liked, Emma." She sneezed and said, "Do you like yours?"

"No. They ask too many questions."

She nodded, wiping her nose on a pink tissue. "Do you answer them?"

"Sometimes. When I want to. Do you?"

She rubbed a hand over her face. "Well, sometimes. When I can."

I looked at the floor, wishing I were anywhere but here. "Yeah. Well, listen, thanks for calling all those people, anyway. You, uh—you didn't take that pill Dad gave you, did you?"

"Of course not. I learned a few things from Ginny too, you know. Did she tell you how much she hated taking pills?"

I shook my head. "No."

"Well, she did. Vitamins or medicine or anything. She was always like that, even when she was still eating. She'd pretend to swallow them and spit them out when she thought I wasn't looking. So that's what I did." She blew her nose and looked down at her lap. "There, you see? I still know more about her than you do."

"I know you do. But six months ago you wouldn't have told anybody she spit out her vitamin pills." My father had told me that women in Mom's family went crazy and got sick and died, but Donna hadn't died from her cancer, and my mother was learning how to live with things that weren't beautiful. I smiled at her and said, "You must have good shrinks, Mom."

She winced. "I'll tell them you said so." We were both silent for a few seconds, and then she said, very quietly, "I still miss her."

"I know," I said, thinking about the lake. "So do I, Mom."

"Emma?"

"What?"

"Don't die. Okay?"

How was I supposed to answer that? Blinking to keep my vision steady, I stared at the white pot and said, "Not any sooner than I have to."

◆ ◇ ◆

For Myrna's sake I kept going to the therapy sessions, although I couldn't see much point to it. Therapy was a charade in which kind people asked me senseless questions to which they, and I, already knew the answers. "How do you feel about your father?" Hateful and furious. "How do you feel about your mother?" Sad and sick. "How do you feel about yourself?" Not great.

It continued like that for months, through the last windy days of autumn and the anniversary of Ginny's death and the first chill, rainy beginnings of spring, until the psychologist—a calm, quiet man serious and unsmiling as an owl, with wire-rimmed glasses and neatly manicured hands—asked me a question about the future, instead of the past: a question that required thought and invention, because I didn't already know the answer.

"Where do you want to be when you grow up?" he asked.

"Huh? I don't know." It was a common enough question, one of those questions everyone's supposed to ask you when you're a kid, but nobody had in a long time, and I hadn't thought about it much. I chewed a nail and stared out the window; it was a lovely day, one of the first warm days of April, when the beauty of the world is still shy and cautious and uncertain. "A park ranger, maybe. Then I could hang around lakes all the time."

He pushed his glasses up farther on his nose, and nodded. "That would be nice, but that's not what I asked you. Where, Emma, not what. Where do you want to be?"

"What?"

"Where," he repeated patiently, not smiling. "Say it's ten years from now: try to picture the place where you'd like to live, and describe it to me."

"I don't know! How am I supposed to answer that?"

"Try. It's not a test."

"Oh, all right." I thought about it. "A big house with lots of people in it. Lots of kids and plants and animals. Dogs and cats and philodendrons and books everyplace, and everything kind of messy, and lots of food around for anyone who wanted it—"

I stopped, as surprised as if I'd caught myself reciting Tennyson. "I want to be Myrna Halloran when I grow up."

My voice cracked when I said it, and that surprised me as much as anything else. Where had all that feeling come from, as unexpected as flowers in January?

◆

But the psychologist only nodded. "Yes. And tell me how you're going to do that."

"I don't know!" He raised an eyebrow and sat back in his chair, and I swallowed in embarrassment. "I don't know if I can."

"I think you can. Tell me how, just a little bit. Anything you know."

I think I can, I think I can. That wasn't one of the books Mom had read me. I squirmed in my seat; I didn't know much. This was worse than a math test.

"I—" I stopped again, profoundly uneasy. "I'll look in the mirror someday and like what I see. That's what Myrna says, anyway. And so somebody else will, too, she says, somebody who's not at all like Dad, but I'm not too clear on that part."

"Stick with yourself. The mirror's good: now what about the house? What else is in it? Who's in it?"

"The people who like the mirror," I said, feeling foolish. "People who love me. Is that possible?"

"Of course it is. People love you now."

"If I get married," I said cautiously, sweating—this was very thin hypothetical ice—"my husband will knock first whenever he enters rooms. Is that possible?"

"Yes," he said positively, and for the first time I noticed the thin gold wedding band on his left hand.

"He'll like lakes, too. Maybe he'll be another ranger; maybe that's how I'll meet him, by looking for people who like lakes." How had Myrna met Tom? I'd have to ask her. "My kids will know how to swim even if they're fat. If I have girls I'll give them baseball bats, and if I have boys they'll have to learn first aid. I'll teach them to grow vegetables. I don't know. This is silly: all I'm doing is telling you about Myrna, and you already know that."

"So do you," he said, "but you don't know that you do. That's why I'm having you say it."

I scowled. He didn't usually sound like a Chinese fortune cookie. He pushed at his glasses again and said mildly, "Tell me about the house again. Myrna has a little room that's just hers, right, where none of the kids can interrupt her? Would you have a room like that?"

"Yeah."

"Good. What's in it?"

I closed my eyes and tried to picture Myrna's sanctuary, and because I knew so little about it I had no choice but to furnish it myself. "Well, it would look out on water or trees, or both. There'd be a big comfortable chair with a reading lamp, and a rolltop desk, Mom's old one from her grandmother—I always liked that—and a little cot for naps. The cats could come in whenever they wanted to, but nobody else could."

"What would you do there?"

"Write letters," I said promptly, my eyes still closed. I could see myself writing letters, sitting at the desk with paper and a pen, and a cat either on my lap or sitting on the paper and trying to play with the pen, the way they do; but who would I be writing to, with the rest of the house filled with all those people? Myrna never had to write letters, because she had everyone she loved around her.

And then I had it. Ginny, yes of course: I'd write letters to Ginny, even though I'd never be able to mail them.

♦

I'd write letters to Ginny and keep them in the rolltop desk. Dear Ginny: We went to Disney World on vacation, and it was really great. Dear Ginny: Today I saw a fox come to the water to drink. I'd have written her a letter when I met the other park ranger, whoever he was, and when we got married and when I had kids. I'd have written her a lot of letters, so she'd understand everything I was doing and how much I wished I could share it with her and how this was the only way I could do that. If I wrote her letters I could give her all the things I wanted to be able to give her, and still have them for myself. I'd have to have them for myself, to give them to her at all.

I'd start writing her letters right away. I'd write her a letter tonight—no, sooner, as soon as I got home. "Dear Ginny: Today I invented the house I want to live in when I grow up."

I opened my eyes, realizing that I hadn't said anything for several minutes. What was the last thing I'd said? "Write letters." And now the mild man opposite me would ask to whom I was writing, and I'd have to tell him about Ginny.

But he just watched me. I took a deep breath. "Do you think," I said, "that I'll be able to do all that?"

He smiled. "Yes, Emma. I know you will."

◆ ◇ ◆

IT WAS long after midnight, and Nancy long asleep, when I finished telling Bret the tale. We'd been interrupted by dinner, by putting Nancy to bed, by Donna calling to invite us to her beach house on Long Island for one last weekend before it got too cold. When I was done with the story Bret hugged me, hard, and held me for a long time, and said "I'm sorry," his voice thick. He'd already known more of it than anyone except Myrna, but even he hadn't known about Ginny. Now he knows all of it.

He's asleep now too. That's his way, not to say much at first, to mull things over and let them settle. I know he'll come back to me in a day or two with questions, with reactions, with his own grief and anger. There's no hurry.

I sit in the study, the door open, and look out at the river, much fainter in moonlight than it was in the afternoon sun. Rivers are roads, my social studies teacher told me fifteen years ago, and I think how the roads Tom built carried me away from home, to Chicago for college and then east, sweeping me to these old worn mountains, where I found a river instead of a lake and an accountant instead of a park ranger; where I became a carpenter and gardener and painter of houses and pictures.

In my own way, I've turned into Myrna, and I know the Halloran clan—now sprawled across the continent, Jane in California and brothers scattered from Texas to Maine, all of them with many children and animals—is proud of me. Hallorans visit whenever they're near, descending in boisterous droves and leaving the house echoing and disordered for days afterwards. My mother would be horrified.

My mother died when I was in college, of a stroke. When I got the news I told myself that she'd be able to rejoin Ginny at last, but even if that's true, it's scant comfort. The two of them are dead, and my father's still alive, still out there somewhere, like toxic waste and nuclear bombs and cancer: all the things that give you nightmares, the fears you grapple with daily and pray your children will never have to face.

Fifteen years later, he still terrifies me. He's inexplicable, the puzzle I've never been able to solve, the cipher I can't decode. My father's sister Diane tried once, four or five years ago, after a decade of her own therapy. She'd written me to ask if she could visit me for an afternoon, and I agreed. I'd never really liked her, but I knew she'd been as horrified as anyone else by what my father had done, and she said in her letter that she'd figured out some things that might help me.

"I keep trying to make sense of it," she told me, sitting stiffly on my living room couch. "Sometimes it seems like I hardly do anything else. And I've remembered a lot. Our father, your dad's and mine, he was mean, Emma. Smart, like your dad, but mean. Boys weren't allowed to cry, you know: your dad got the belt if he cried, and got it hard, too, and our mother went along with it because she thought that was what wives did."

She looked at me, her face anguished, and said, "Your father's first piece of surgery, when he was a very little boy, was to cut away all his feelings. And he never managed to sew them back on again. I don't think he can feel pain anymore, or much of anything else. Other people are—they're like artificial limbs for him, you understand? He can make them feel things he can't feel himself. I remember how he loved biology lab, in high school. Sticking pins in frogs, cutting them up and getting A's for it. He could be as mean to those frogs as our dad had been to him, and his teachers would praise him for doing it so well."

"Nobody asked the frogs," I said.

"No. But when you're a doctor, people ask you to cut them up. They're grateful to you for cutting them up, because you're also keeping them alive. So even though you're hurting them, they pay you lots of money for it and tell you how important you are."

"Oranges," I said.

"What?"

"Never mind. Go on."

"So—well, I think your father struck a bargain with himself: I think he told himself that it was all right to hurt people, as long as he helped them too. And I think he felt that way about—about his family. Because he was supporting you, keeping a roof over your head. I'm not defending him, believe me. Just trying to make sense of it."

"I saw him cry once," I said. "Talking about Ginny."

Diane nodded. "He fell apart when she died. He'd always hated losing patients. It made him so angry—and now I think that was really guilt, underneath, because he hadn't kept up his end of this bargain. Maybe I'm wrong. But when Ginny died—oh, it tore him apart, Emma. I don't know if I can make you believe that. I don't think he believed it himself, and it was so long since he'd felt anything, really felt anything, that he didn't know what to do. So he got drunk, and there was that scene with Donna."

"I think he did the same thing to Ginny he did to me," I told her. I didn't want to tell her about Ginny's ghost. "It would explain a lot."

"I know," Diane said, and dug a tissue out of her purse and sniffled for a little while. "I hope—I hope I've done you some good, telling you all this. It's helped me, understanding that much." She finished wiping her face and said, "I had nightmares for months after the trial. I guess we all did. I guess you probably still do. But I'd always been so proud of Stewart, and suddenly I was terrified of turning into him."

"Why didn't you? You had the same parents."

"I was a girl," she said simply. "I was allowed to cry. Girls were supposed to be weak, you see, so our dad didn't hit me as often as he hit Stewart." She laughed once, harshly. It was a sound my father might have made. "And now—well, now I boss horses around."

I don't know how much of Diane's theory I believe, how much it really explains. I worry about the little girls who live where my father does. Diane says he's avoided children since the trial, and I hope she's right. I've learned to live with his freedom, as I live with the danger of rockslides and flash flooding from spring storms. He doesn't know where I am, and no one who does is likely to tell him. I have a different name now, a different life. It wouldn't be easy for him to find me.

And even if he did, he'd never get his hands on

Nancy. I can't protect every child in the world, but I can protect my own. If he tried to touch her, I know I'd kill him. That hard, chill certainty comforts me almost as much as it frightens.

The ceiling above me creaks: Bret turning in bed upstairs, and the old house letting me know about it. Time to join him, and let the even flow of his breathing send me off to sleep.

Tomorrow I'll tell Ginny that I've told someone else I love. I know I left her behind a long time ago, in my journey through a succession of landscapes she'd never recognize, and perhaps one day I'll abandon the charade and just keep a journal, the way everyone else does. But not yet. "I'm as real as you are," she told me, the first time I saw her. Somewhere, she still is.